Noodlehead
STORIES
World Tales Kids Can Read & Tell

Noodlehead
STORIES
World Tales Kids Can Read & Tell

Retold by Martha Hamilton and Mitch Weiss
Beauty and the Beast Storytellers

Illustrations by Ariane Elsammak

August House Publishers, Inc.
LITTLE ROCK

Printed in the United States of America
10 9 8 7 6 5 4 3 2 1   HC
10 9 8 7 6 5 4 3 2 1   PB

LIBRARY OF CONGRESS CATALOGING-IN-PUBLICATION DATA
Noodlehead stories : world tales kids can read & tell / retold by
Martha Hamilton and Mitch Weiss ; illustrations by Arian Elsammak.
    p.   cm.
Includes bibliographical references.
Summary: A collection of folktales from around the world, all featuring the character
of the fool, with tips for telling the stories aloud, related activities, and source notes.
ISBN 0-87483-584-4 (alk. paper) —
ISBN 0-87483-585-2 (pbk. : alk. paper)
1. Tales. [1. Folklore. 2. Storytelling—Collections.]
I. Hamilton, Martha. II. Weiss, Mitch. III. Elsammak, Ariane, ill.
PZ8.1 .N74   2000
398.2—dc21   00-056602

Executive editor: Liz Parkhurst
Project editor: Joy Freeman
Copyeditor: Jenny Counts
Cover and interior illustration: Ariane Elsammak
Cover and book design: Joy Freeman

The paper used in this publication meets the minimum requirements
of the American National Standard for Information Sciences—
Permanence of Paper for Printed Library Materials, ANSI Z39.48-1984.

AUGUST HOUSE, INC.   PUBLISHERS   LITTLE ROCK

With love to all the noodleheads in our lives.
You know who you are.

Acknowledgments

Thanks to the kids who listened to and told these stories. Your enthusiasm made us want to find more "noodlehead" stories and eventually led us to write this book. We are very grateful to those who read the manuscript and offered suggestions: Karen Baum, June Locke, Hope and Max Mandeville, Christina Stark, and Coley and Will Weinstein. Others who lent a hand in one way or another were: Allen J. Riedy, Patrick Ryan, Nancy Skipper, and the reference staff at Tompkins County Public Library who made every effort to fill our seemingly unending inter-library loan requests. And special thanks for the support from the folks at August House. From the chief noodle down to the lowly intern who, with a stroke of genius, created "real" noodleheads for promotional purposes—you're all great fun to work with! Joy, your spirit and talent are very much appreciated!

Contents

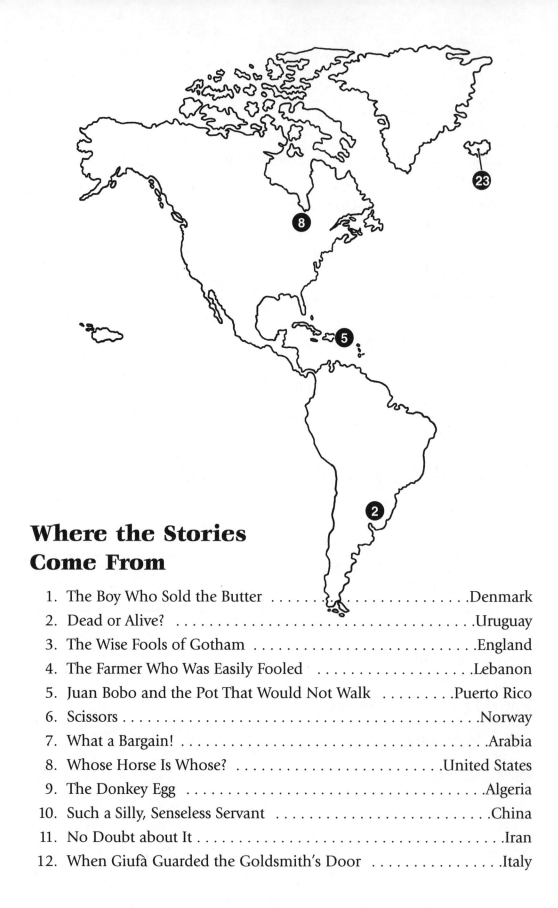

Where the Stories Come From

Introduction

What's a noodlehead? A person who doesn't use his brains, so much so that his head appears to be filled with noodles. World folklore is rich with stories of fools. Because we've all been caught not using our brains at one time or another, everyone enjoys a good numskull tale. It reminds us we're not alone when we hear a story in which someone *else* is the fool!

We believe we have good qualifications to write a book about noodleheads. Although we could probably fill a book with our *own* noodlehead stories, we'll just give you two examples. Mitch once locked his keys in the car—*with the car running!* Martha once asked someone, "What time is the eight o'clock meeting?" Everyone can find comfort in the old Jewish saying, "All wise people act foolishly sometimes."

Numskull tales have been told for as long as people have been telling stories. In 1888, W.A. Clouston wrote a book called *The Book of Noodles*. In it he described numerous stories that had been told for hundreds of years with quite a few dating back over two millenia! In all that time, people have never tired of telling noodle tales—they just dressed them up in new clothes. Clouston also pointed out that people around the world told the same noodle stories. If a story was told about the Italian fool, Giufà, it was most likely told about Juan Bobo in Puerto Rico and Jack in England and the United States, as well. People may have primarily told these stories for entertainment, but we can learn much about human nature by reading and telling them.

What makes people look foolish? Some fools are very well meaning. Like Jack in "Next Time I'll Know What to Do," they follow directions carefully, thinking they are being clever, but never once use their brains. Some fools, such as Clever Elsie, look for the most complicated solution to a very simple problem. Even worse, some noodleheads, such as the two in the story "Whose Horse is Whose?" create a problem that doesn't exist.

Fools can be young or old, rich or poor, weak or powerful. They can be male or female, but there are many more numskull stories where men are the main characters. Sometimes there is a "village fool." Other times, such as in Chelm or Gotham, there is a whole village of fools. In some of the stories we feel like we might know the people and the setting. In others, the stories leap into an absurd world of the totally impossible.

Noodlehead stories are often quite farfetched. The characters think they are someone else when they wear another person's clothes or believe they are dead when they are quite alive! What a comfort to think that we just do small foolish things now and then, while others are capable of such lunacy.

There is an old saying, "Fortune, that favors fools." The people of the world who told these noodle tales seemed to have a great desire that all should be well for the simpleton. For example, in spite of his foolishness, the noodlehead in "The Boy Who Sold the Butter" is rewarded at the end of the story with great wealth. Perhaps it's a reflection of the fact that life isn't fair, that there really is such a thing as "fool's luck." But we think there's another reason such stories were told. The boy respects his mother, listens to her advice, and follows her directions carefully. Maybe the point was that even the most foolish can achieve good if they will only follow the wisdom of their elders.

These noodle stories are not meant to be told for the purpose of making fun of others, but rather in the spirit of laughing at the noodlehead in all of us. Remember that, as the French humorist François Rabelais once said, "If you wish to avoid seeing a fool, you must first break your mirror." We have avoided using words such as "stupid" or "dumb" since they are used to criticize or belittle others, and hope you will take care with the words you choose if you decide to tell these stories. Instead, use humorous words such as "noodlehead," "numskull," "nincompoop," or "ninnyhammer."

The tales in this book are fun to read to yourself or out loud to someone else, and they are especially fun to tell. In case you're interested, we've included tips for telling each story *without* the book.

Remember that there are many ways to tell a story. Our tips are merely suggestions. Your way of telling the tale may be completely different but work just as well or even better. We've also included a chapter with general storytelling tips.

We've found that hearing or reading these stories often gives kids (and adults) great ideas for making up and telling *their own* stories. For those who need a creative jumpstart, we've provided a list of suggested activities at the end of the book.

Our job for the last twenty years has been telling stories and teaching kids and adults to tell stories. We've found that kids (and adults) are usually nervous and a bit hesitant to tell their first tale. But once they get started, there's often no stopping them. As one third grade storyteller wrote after telling her story to a large group of classmates and parents, "At first, I had butterflies and jitterbugs in my whole body! I said to myself, 'I'm going to have to pick an easy story.' But instead I picked a hard one that I really liked. Before I told my story, I felt like I wouldn't be able to talk, but then the butterflies and jitterbugs died completely. The story came out, and at the end I felt great. I feel like my whole life changed when I was able to get up in front of everyone."

Telling a story is scary at first, but it's a great feeling to see the delight in the eyes of your listeners and to hear them applaud afterward. So no matter what your age, go on. Take a chance. Read these stories and then pass them along. Like a good joke, people just can't get enough of these noodlehead stories. They're sure to bring a smile to the lips of your listeners and perhaps, if you're lucky, a funny tale as well. Say, did you hear the one about the fool who taught his horse to go without food? He was terribly upset because, after weeks of training, the horse up and died…

The Boy Who Sold the Butter

A Story from Denmark

There was once a woman who had a noodlehead for a son. When he helped with the chores on the farm, he usually made a mess of things, so she found it easier to do most of the work herself.

One morning, she churned a big pot of sweet butter that she planned to sell in town. Her son begged, "Mother, please let me take the butter to town to sell."

"No," said his mother. "You've never even been to town. It's big, and you'll get lost. Stay home and keep the cow company." But he pleaded with her for so long that she finally agreed. She gave him some advice on how to sell the butter, and off he went.

He followed the road just as his mother had told him. After what seemed like a very long time, he came upon an enormous rock. He thought, "My mother said the town was big. This certainly is big. It must be the town!" So he said to the rock, "Town, would you like to buy some of my mother's butter?"

The rock, of course, didn't answer. It was a rock, after all. This didn't stop the boy. He went right on talking. He was a noodlehead, after all.

"Ohhhhh! My mother has told me about people like you. You won't buy something until you've tried it. No problem. Here's a sample for you." With that, he smeared some butter on the rock. Since it was a hot day, it wasn't long before the sun melted the butter.

"Ohhhhh!" said the noodlehead, "I can tell by how quickly you ate it that you loved my mother's butter. I guess that means you'd like to buy the rest of it. Well, I'd be glad to sell it to you." Then the boy smeared the rest of the butter on the rock, and it quickly melted.

"Now, town, if you'll just pay me for the butter, I'll be on my way."

The rock said nothing.

"Ohhhhh! My mother says the smartest people are the ones who use the fewest words. Don't worry. You don't have to say a thing. Just give me the money, and I won't bother you anymore."

There was no reply. The boy was beginning to get angry. He raised his voice a bit. "Now, town, listen to me. *You* ate the butter, so *I* must have my money."

When the rock *still* didn't answer, the boy began to kick and shove it until suddenly the rock rolled over. And in a hole under the rock there sat…a big pot filled with gold!

Being a noodlehead, the boy didn't realize his good luck. He said, "Thank you, town! I knew you would pay me for the butter."

The boy took the money home, and after that he and his mother lived in comfort for the rest of their lives.

About the story

The theme of a person selling goods to an object is a common one in world folklore. A similar story is told of the Italian fool, Giufà. He sells clothing to a statue and then hits the statue when it doesn't pay. The statue breaks apart to reveal a treasure, and Giufà thinks the statue has paid him. For a different Giufà story, read "When Giufà Guarded the Goldsmith's Door" on page 47.

Tips for telling

When the boy begs his mother to let him go to town, pretend that you are the boy and your listeners are his mother. Bend down slightly as he begs to take the butter to town and look right at the audience. Then, when you speak as his mother, you may want to straighten your body and put your hands on your hips when she says, "No! You stay home and keep the cow company!"

When the boy sees the rock, pretend that you really see it with your eyes. Scratch your head and look very confused as he says, "My mother said the town was big..." Each time the boy says, "Ohhhhh!" stretch that word out and say it as if you've just had a brainstorm. Sound very angry when the boy realizes he's not going to get his payment. At the end, pause right after the rock rolls over. Pretend to see the pot of gold and look very excited before you tell your listeners what he found under the rock.

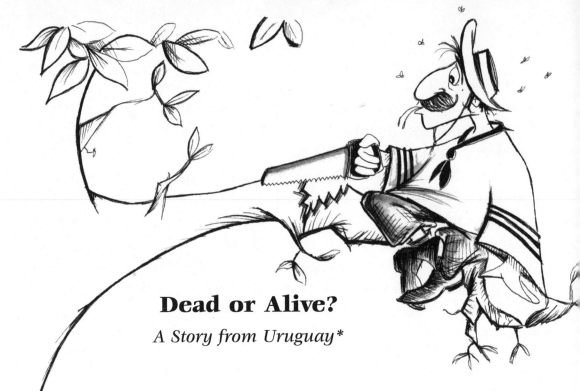

Dead or Alive?

A Story from Uruguay*

A fool went out to cut wood for a fire. He grabbed a saw, climbed a tree, and sat on a sturdy limb. Then he started sawing the very limb he was *sitting* on. Zzzzz Zzzzzz Zzzzz.

Just then a woman walked by and noticed him up in the tree. "Stop!" she cried. "If you keep sawing, that branch will fall, and you'll fall and hurt yourself. Stop!"

"Why doesn't she mind her own business?" thought the fool. He ignored her and kept on sawing. Zzzzz Zzzzzz Zzzzz. The woman threw up her hands and went on her way.

Before long, *crack!* The limb broke, and the fool tumbled to the ground. "*Ohhhhh*, that hurts!" cried the fool as he lay on the ground. But then he thought, "Wait a minute! That woman said that branch would fall. Sure enough, it did fall! She said I would fall. Sure enough, I did fall! She also said I'd hurt myself. Sure enough, I did! That woman must be a fortune-teller. I'll go find her so she can tell me more about my future." The fool hurried down the trail until he caught up with her.

"You are a good fortune-teller," he told

* Uruguay is pronounced YOUR-eh-gway.

the woman. "Can you predict everything that will happen?"

"Oh, not *everything*," she replied. She knew there was no point trying to explain that she wasn't a fortune-teller to such a noodlehead.

"Can you tell me when I'll die?" asked the fool.

The woman answered with the first idea that popped into her head. "Yes. You will die when your donkey drinks three times along the road."

"Thanks for warning me," said the fool.

The next day the fool had to go to a nearby village. He set off on his donkey, not remembering what the woman had told him. As it was a hot day, his donkey naturally stopped to take a drink when they crossed a small creek. The fool thought nothing of it until they came to another creek and his donkey once again took a drink. He suddenly remembered the woman's prediction. "Oh no!" he cried. "One more drink, and I'm a goner!"

After awhile, they came to a brook. Before the fool could stop her, his donkey leaned down and took a third drink. The fool cried, "Well, I guess that's it. I'm dead." He got off the donkey and lay down on the ground. He held his arms stiff at his sides and closed his eyes.

Since there was no shortage of fools in these parts, it wasn't surprising that two more nincompoops happened to pass by. When they saw the fool lying on the ground, one said, "Look at this poor fellow. He must be dead."

"How can you tell?" asked the other.

"You knucklehead!" he replied. "It's obvious—his eyes are closed."

"Oh. That's a good point. Well, I guess we'd better go get a coffin and bury him in the graveyard."

The two men left and then returned a bit later with a coffin. They put the fool in it, picked up the coffin, and headed toward the graveyard. When they came to a fork in the road, they argued about which was the correct way. "Go to the left!" said one. "Go to the right!" yelled the other. They argued back and forth.

"Left!"

"Right!"

"Left!"

"Right!"

At last, the "dead" fool spoke up. "Excuse me! When I was alive, I always went to the left."

When the two ninnyhammers heard this, they squealed, "Oh no! This dead man talks! He must have already turned into a *ghost!*" They screamed, dropped the coffin, and scurried off.

As for the fool, he laid in the coffin until nightfall. Then he got up and went home. He was never the same after that. Perhaps the fall knocked some sense into him, for afterwards he seemed to use his brain more than he ever had before.

About the story

The notion that someone could actually convince another person that he's dead is perhaps the most farfetched of all the noodlehead story plots we encountered in our research, yet this theme is often found in world folktales. Another story with this theme, "I'd Laugh, Too, If I Weren't Dead," can be found on page 76.

Tips for telling

Pretend to saw a branch to your side and make a sawing noise if you feel comfortable doing so. When the woman tells him to stop, look up as if you're talking to the fool in the tree.

After the fool falls to the ground, sound amazed as he realizes that each thing the woman warned him about came true. Later on, when he thinks he has died and lies down, put your arms to your side, look very stiff, and close your eyes for a second. The two fools who carry the coffin should sound terrified when they think the "dead" man has turned into a ghost.

The Wise Fools of Gotham

A Story from England

There's a small town in the central part of England called Gotham.*
Some say it's a town of fools. Others say all the villagers are wise. Let me
tell you about the people of Gotham so you can decide for yourself.

Long ago, England was ruled by a cruel king named John. One day,
the people of Gotham heard that King John and his men would soon
be riding through their town. This worried the villagers, for they knew the
greedy king would demand food and lodging
for his men. What's more, if he saw anything
to his liking, he would surely take it.

A town meeting was called. After
much discussion, the townspeople
decided to cut down a number of
huge trees to block the roads leading
into Gotham. When King John and
his men reached the outskirts of the
village, they could not pass. Enraged,
King John ordered his men to go into
the town and punish the villagers.

When the king's officers finally made
their way over the trees, they found a
village of fools. Some say that was
because the people of Gotham had a
plan—they had decided to act like fools
since they had never heard of anyone
being punished for being a noodlehead. Others say that's just the way
they were.

* Gotham is pronounced GOTH-am.

In the village, the king's men encountered a man riding a donkey. The man was hunched over because he carried a huge sack of grain on his own shoulders. He looked exhausted. One of the king's men approached him and asked, "Why, in heaven's name, are you carrying that sack? Why don't you just put it behind you on your donkey's back?"

"You see," replied the man from Gotham, "my donkey is feeling poorly today. It's bad enough that she has to carry me, so I decided to lighten her burden by carrying the sack myself."

The king's men said, "But sir, don't you see that if you're riding on top of the donkey, she's still carrying the weight of the sack?"

The man didn't reply. He just looked at the king's men as if *they* were crazy and went on his way.

The king's officers giggled at the foolishness of the man. Before long, they passed a pond where they found a number of villagers in the midst of a great argument. Two of them were holding an enormous eel. "Quiet down," commanded one of the king's men. "What's the problem here?"

One of the villagers stepped forward and said, "Last year we took all the extra fish we caught and put them in this pond so they would multiply. But this year when we came back, all we caught was this one huge eel. Obviously it has eaten all of our fish! Since then, we have argued long and hard over how to punish this wicked eel. But we have finally agreed on the perfect punishment. We are just about to drown the eel in this very pond!"

The king's officers couldn't believe their ears. Drown an eel whose home is in the water? These men were sillier than the first man they met!

Before long, they reached the center of the village, where they were in for another surprise. There they found the rest of the townspeople building a towering stone wall. When the soldiers inquired what was going on, one of the villagers replied, "Every spring a cuckoo comes to live in our village. It always brings warm weather. When it leaves, the cold weather returns. Last year we decided that if we could get the cuckoo to stay here all year, we would always have warm weather. We built this stone wall, but it obviously wasn't high enough because the bird flew away. This year we're determined to build it so high that the cuckoo can't escape."

The king's officers had heard enough. They couldn't bring themselves to punish such nincompoops. They returned to King John and told him all about the fools of Gotham. Whether it's fair or not, the people of Gotham have been known as fools ever since.

What do you think? Were the villagers of Gotham wise or foolish?

About the story

King John ruled England from 1199 until 1216. The legendary Robin Hood supposedly fought against the cruel king and his officers. The Magna Carta or Great Charter was signed in 1215 as a response to John's cruel reign. It placed the king under English law and reduced his power.

The earliest *written* reference to the tales of the fools of Gotham dates back to 1450. The king's officers actually met many more foolish Gothamites. We have described only three of the incidents. However, many of the other stories in this book were also told about the fools of Gotham. For example, one story was of twelve Gothamites who couldn't count themselves, which is similar to the French tale "Seven Foolish Fishermen" on page 58.

Tips for telling

At the beginning when you say "some say," make a hand gesture to one side. When you say, "others say," make a motion toward the other side as if to show the opposite viewpoint.

The king's officers should grow more and more amazed each time they meet a fool or group of fools in Gotham. Show with your voice and face that the officers just can't believe the Gothamites could be so foolish. On the other hand, be sure to convey that the Gothamites have the same feeling toward the officers. They are just as convinced that *their* way of doing things is best.

The Farmer Who Was Easily Fooled

*A Story from Lebanon**

At the end of a long day at the market, a farmer headed home. He led his donkey, which was tied to a rope, behind him. He didn't realize he was being watched by two dishonest men at the side of the road.

"I know that farmer," said one of the thieves. "He isn't very clever. I'll bet I can steal his donkey right now without him knowing it."

"In broad daylight?" asked the other. "How could you possibly do that?"

"Just come with me, and I'll show you," he replied.

The two thieves crept up behind the farmer, who was so tired he didn't notice. The first thief untied the rope from the donkey's neck and tied it around his own. Then he motioned for his companion to lead the donkey out of sight.

The thief continued to walk along behind the farmer. But as soon as the other thief and the donkey were safely hidden, he stopped. The farmer gave a little jerk on his rope to encourage his donkey, but the thief didn't move. The farmer turned around to scold his donkey and was stunned to see a man in the donkey's place. "Who are you? And what happened to my donkey?"

The thief replied, "I know this is hard to believe, but *I* am your donkey!" The foolish farmer didn't know what to think. "But how is that possible?"

"Let me explain," said the thief. "As a young man, I caused great trouble for my poor mother. I lied. I gambled. I never did anything she asked me to do. One day, she was so furious that she shouted, 'Oh, I wish you were turned into a donkey!' And at that very instant, I was. I have stayed in the form of a donkey for years until just now, when the spell finally wore off. Thank goodness I'm a man again."

* Lebanon is pronounced LEHB-ah-nahn.

"That's an amazing story," said the farmer. "But it makes me feel terrible. I apologize for the harsh way I treated you. I should never have loaded you down so."

"That's fine," replied the thief. "It was all part of the lesson I needed to learn. Now I must go and apologize to my mother for the way I treated her."

"Here, take this to help you get started in your new life as a man," said the foolish farmer. He gave the thief all the money he had made at the market that day. "I'm sure you'll change your ways after all you've been through. Now, go home to your mother."

With that, the farmer and the thief parted ways. After a good laugh, the two thieves went to town and sold the donkey at the market.

The following day, the farmer returned to the market to buy a new donkey. To his surprise, one of the donkeys for sale seemed familiar. When he looked carefully, he realized it was his old donkey!

"Is it possible?" he shrieked. "After only one day of freedom, you've already made your mother so angry that she turned you back into a donkey! Won't you ever learn your lesson? Well, I'm certainly not going to buy you. Maybe your next master won't be as kind as I was."

With that, the foolish farmer bought a different donkey and returned home.

About the story

The farmer in this story believes everything he hears without questioning. All of us have believed something someone told us until he said "Just kidding!" and we realized how silly we were to believe it in the first place. This story reminds us that if something sounds too far-fetched or too good to be true, it probably is.

Tips for telling

Look and sound stunned when the farmer finds the man in his donkey's place. Make the thief sound very convincing when he tells his story. At the end, when the farmer returns to the market to buy a new donkey, show surprise when he recognizes his old one. Then sound extremely angry when the farmer scolds the donkey for disobeying his mother.

Juan Bobo and the Pot
That Would Not Walk

A Story from Puerto Rico

On the island of Puerto Rico they tell stories of a boy named Juan*
Bobo. This is the Spanish name for "Foolish John." In all the stories,
Juan Bobo means well. But though his heart is full of kindness, his
head seems to be empty. Here's one story they like to tell about him.

Juan Bobo lived with his mother in a little cottage at the foot of a
hill. One day, she started to make a chicken and rice stew but didn't
have a pot big enough. So she called for Juan Bobo and said, "Juan
Bobo, go to your grandmother's and borrow her biggest pot. Hurry
along now, so I can get our dinner ready."

Juan Bobo bounded up the hill toward his grandmother's house.
He was happy to help, especially since he knew his mother was making his favorite meal. His grandmother gladly gave him the pot. It was
an old-fashioned iron pot with three legs. Juan Bobo lifted it up onto
his shoulder and set off. But the pot was heavy. Soon sweat began to
drip down Juan Bobo's forehead. His shoulder ached. So he put the
pot on the ground and sat down to rest a bit.

As Juan Bobo looked at the pot, he thought, "That pot has three
legs! I have only two. Why should *I* break my back carrying *it?*"

Then he spoke to the pot with an angry tone, "Walk on down to my
house, you lazy, good-for-nothing pot. Let's have a race. I should get a
head start since you have three legs, and I have only two." Then Juan
Bobo told the pot exactly where his cottage was and ran on down the hill.

When Juan Bobo burst in the door, he asked breathlessly, "Did I
beat the pot, or is it already here?"

---

* Juan is pronounced WAN. It sounds just like "wand" (as in magic wand) but
  without the "d" at the end.

His mother had no time for such foolishness. "Juan Bobo, *what* are you talking about? How could the pot have gotten here without you carrying it?"

"Haven't you noticed, mother? That pot has good strong legs. Three of them, in fact. So I told it to walk home."

"Oh, Juan Bobo!" said his mother. "Pots can't walk. Now, go back up the hill and fetch that pot!"

Juan Bobo trudged back up the hill. Of course, he found the pot just where he had left it. "You lazy pot!" yelled Juan Bobo. "You just sat there and let me get into trouble with my mother! How selfish of you. Now, I'll give you one last chance. It's time to cook dinner, and you're needed at my house, so get going!"

When the pot still didn't move, Juan Bobo grew even angrier. He kicked the pot, and it tipped over and began to roll down the hill. Juan Bobo called out, "It's a good thing you finally came to your senses and listened to me!"

That night Juan Bobo and his mother enjoyed a tasty chicken and rice stew. The next morning, Juan Bobo's mother asked him to return the pot.

Juan Bobo begged the pot to go back up the hill. When it didn't move, he pointed his finger at it and warned, "All right, pot. I guess you're too tired from cooking last night. I'll carry you up the hill this time, but don't expect this treatment again!"

There's no telling what happened the next time Juan Bobo had to fetch the pot. But one thing is certain. Whatever he did, he always lived up to the name of 'Juan Bobo.'

About the story

Juan Bobo stories are told not only in Puerto Rico but also in the Caribbean Islands and in many South American countries. This same tale of the three-legged pot is also told in England. One of the fools of Gotham* buys a pot at the market. He grows weary of carrying it, notices it has three legs, tells it how to get to his house, and demands that it walk there. When he gets home and tells his wife the story, she's afraid it will be stolen. Her husband is convinced that the pot will be coming along any time. In the end, his wife goes to retrieve the pot.

Tips for telling

Use body movements to show how Juan Bobo lifts the pot and carries it on his shoulder and then puts it down when it grows heavy. Each time he scolds the pot, pretend to grow angry and point your finger at it. Use body language to show the difference between Juan Bobo and his mother.

*For another story about the fools of Gotham, see page 23.

Scissors

A Story from Norway

There was once a woman who loved to argue. No matter what anyone else said, she always said the opposite. As a result, most people in her village tried to look the other way when they saw her coming. They knew they were in for some kind of disagreement. If the butcher offered her lamb chops, she wanted pork chops. If a farmer had beets to sell, she'd surely ask, "Don't you have any turnips?"

It was her husband, of course, who had to put up with most of her foolishness. If he opened a window, she would shut it. If he shut it, she would open it. If he said, "Why, look, it's raining outside," she would reply, "It looks like snow to me."

One day, they were out working in their fields when the husband said, "It looks as if the corn will be ready to harvest by Wednesday." But his wife replied, "What? It won't be ready until Thursday."

"All right, Thursday," replied her husband, trying to be agreeable. "I'll get several children from the village to help us."

"No, you won't," said his wife. "We'll do it ourselves."

"Very well," replied her husband, "doing it ourselves will be good since it will save us some money. And another good thing—I think the weather will be perfect."

"No, it won't!" snapped his wife." It's going to rain. I can feel it in my bones."

At this point the husband was losing his patience, but he replied as sweetly as possible, "Dear, let's not argue over every little detail. There is one thing we can certainly agree on. We will cut the corn with scythes.*"

Much to his amazement, his wife replied, "No, this year, just for a change, we will cut the corn with scissors!"

Finally, the husband lost his temper and shouted, "Have you gone mad? No one harvests corn that way. If we use scissors, we'll have to bend down and cut one stalk at a time. But with the long sharp blade of a scythe, we will be able to cut a whole section with one swing. We will cut the corn with *scythes!*"

"You heard me the first time," said his wife. "We will cut the corn with *scissors!*"

The argument went back and forth.

"Scythes!"

"Scissors!"

"Scythes!"

"Scissors!"

Finally, the woman stomped off toward home. But she wasn't looking where she was going. She tripped on a rock and tumbled into the river that ran beside their cornfield. Her husband rushed to save her, but when her head came up, she was too stubborn to cry for help. Instead, she continued their argument. "Scissors!" she shouted.

"Scythes!" he called out just before she dipped below the surface.

When her head bobbed up again, she shouted, "Scissors!"

"Scythes!" replied her husband, as he watched her head disappear below the water.

She came up one last time. But this time her mouth was so full of water that she couldn't say a word. All her husband could see was her hand above the water and her fingers going snip-snip as if to shout "Scissors!" Then she was gone.

"That stubborn woman! What a stubborn, bullheaded woman!" he groaned.

He ran back to the village to get his neighbors to help him find his wife, but they didn't have any luck. Then, one of the neighbors said, "If

---

* A scythe is a tool used long ago for mowing grass. It has a long handle that is attached to a long curving blade for cutting. Scythe is pronounced SITH. It's as if you say the word "sigh" (rhymes with pie) and add "th" at the end of it.

33

the water has carried her away, she'll be downstream. That's the way the river flows." So they went downstream and looked, but she was nowhere to be found.

At last her husband said, "What a fool I am! We're looking in the wrong place. It's true that anyone else would float downstream. But not *my* wife! She'll do just the opposite. She's going upstream, for sure."

They ran along the riverbank, heading upstream. There, just as the man had guessed, they found his wife, going against the current. What's more, she was headed *up* a waterfall!

With one last shout of "Scissors!" the stubborn woman disappeared over the top of the waterfall and was never seen again.

About the story

Stubbornness is certainly a trait that can make people look very foolish. In one well-known story from India, a husband and wife both refuse to close the door when the wind blows it open. They agree that whoever speaks first will close it. As the two sit in silence, a thief, who has overheard their bet, walks in and begins to steal their belongings. They both remain silent until he picks up a box full of money, and then the husband and wife speak at the same time. When the thief runs off with their valuables, rather than chase him, they continue their argument about closing the door!

Tips for telling

Use hand motions to show how contrary the woman is. For example, when you say, "If the butcher offered her lamb chops," gesture to your left, and then to your right when you say, "She wanted pork chops" (or vice versa). Each time the woman speaks, sound very headstrong. Put your hands on your hips or fold your arms across your chest. At the beginning, when the husband speaks, slump your shoulders a bit to show that he doesn't agree with her but is trying to be agreeable. When the husband loses his patience and begins to argue as well, it may become more difficult to show the difference between the two. Practice in a mirror until you can convincingly show with your body that two different people are arguing back and forth.

What a Bargain!

A Story from Arabia*

In Arabia, long ago, a husband and wife lived in a small, tumble-down shack. They had many ideas about how to make money, but they never seemed to have any. The reason was obvious to everyone else in their village—they were both noodleheads.

One morning, the husband looked at their crumbling cottage and said, "Our home is falling to pieces. We've got to find a way to get some money to repair it."

"Oh, that's not a problem," replied his wife. "You take our cow to market to sell. She's worth at least ten coins. I have some extra thread I can sell. Between the two of us, we'll easily make enough to repair our house."

The husband agreed, and together they set off for the market.

Once there, he gave the cow to the man in charge of selling animals. Since a lot of people were standing around, the salesman tried to sell the cow at once. He called out: "Everyone, look at this excellent cow! She gives delicious milk. She eats very little for her size. She's in the best of health. You won't find a better cow anywhere. Who'll give me ten coins for her?"

"I'll bid ten!" yelled one of the men in the crowd.

"Eleven!" shouted another.

The noodlehead was amazed to hear his cow described in such glowing terms and to have people bidding on her without hesitation. He thought to himself, "Why, she truly is a fine cow. I can't let my prize cow

* Arabia is a peninsula in the southwestern part of Asia. It consists of Saudi Arabia, Yemen, Oman, and Kuwait.

go to someone else." He took out his money and counted fifteen coins.

"Fifteen!" he cried out.

"Sold," shouted the salesman. And much to the amazement of the crowd, the foolish man paid fifteen coins for his *own* cow.

The man hurried to find his wife and said, "Dear, you won't believe how clever I am. Let me tell you about the bargain I got!"

"First, I must tell you about the shrewd bargain I just made," replied his wife. "Then we can decide who is more clever."

"All right," agreed the husband. "Go on, if you must."

"Well, dear, I quickly found a buyer for my thread. He praised its quality but wanted to weigh it before paying my price of five coins. It didn't weigh as much as he thought, and he was about to back out of our deal. But I suddenly had a brilliant idea. When he wasn't looking, I took my silver bracelet and slipped it in among the thread. Then, I told him to weigh it again. This time he was pleased and paid my full price. He never even knew that he took home my bracelet as well."

The husband praised his wife's quick thinking and then told her what had happened to him. "Oh, husband," she replied. "It is fortunate that we are both so clever. When we put our brains together, we can solve any problem."

Afterwards, they did wonder why, in spite of their cleverness, they seemed to have less money than before. Perhaps they've repaired their little house by now, but if they haven't, it hardly matters. For the two noodleheads still have their cow…and each other.

About the story

We found a similar story from Idaho where a farmer took his cow to an auction and ended up buying it himself. As for the wife, she's not only a noodlehead but also dishonest. She thinks she's cheating the man, but she's actually cheating herself since a silver bracelet is much more valuable than thread. This brings to mind a news report we saw recently about a noodlehead thief. A man stole a six pack of soda and was recorded by the surveillance camera. He was arrested when he returned a few hours later to get the five-cent deposit for each bottle! This certainly proves that noodleheads are alive and well today.

Tips for telling

When the salesman is trying to sell the cow, show great enthusiasm. Point toward the side as you pretend to show the imaginary cow to the audience. When the man shouts, "I'll bid ten!" look very excited and hold up one hand the way people do at auctions.

When the wife tells her husband how she sold the thread, make her sound very proud and pleased with herself. Make a hand gesture when she explains how she slipped the silver bracelet in among the thread. It's important to say that it was a silver bracelet so that your listeners know the bracelet is valuable and will understand how foolish she has been.

Whose Horse Is Whose?

A Story from the Midwestern United States

There were two noodleheads who loved to go horseback riding together. However, they did have one problem. They had an awful time trying to tell their horses apart.

One of the fools decided to solve the problem by cutting off part of his horse's mane. That worked fine. Now they had no trouble telling their horses apart. But eventually the mane grew back in, and they were right back where they started.

Then the other fool had an idea. He cut off part of his horse's tail. That worked well, too. Now one horse had a short tail, and the other a long tail. But one day, the other horse got his tail caught in a fence, and it had to be cut free. Now the tails were the same length. So, again, they couldn't tell their horses apart.

At this point, the fools were ready to give up. Then one of the noodleheads said, "Wait! Why don't we measure our horses?" The other one replied, "Now that's a brilliant idea." So they took a yardstick and carefully measured each horse. They were amazed to find that the brown horse was three inches taller than the white one with black spots.

The noodleheads praised themselves for finally coming up with a solution to their problem. After that, they had no trouble telling their horses apart.

About the story

Noodleheads sometimes create problems where they don't exist. If we look at this story logically, it seems it would have been impossible for this to happen unless the two fools never opened their eyes. Even though the story couldn't really be "true," there's a lot of truth to be found in it. The story makes the point that sometimes the answer to a problem is really right in front of us. We don't notice the obvious because we aren't really paying attention.

Tips for telling

Use hand motions to show the fools cutting off one horse's tail and then the other one's mane. Show great frustration each time they end up back where they started. When one fool says, "Wait! Why don't we measure our horses?" say it as if it is the most brilliant idea anyone has ever thought of. After they measure them, sound truly amazed and gesture with your hands toward one side as you say "the brown horse" and then toward the other as you say "the white one with black spots."

The Donkey Egg

A Story from Algeria*

There was once a boy who was very foolish. In fact, he was a real noodlehead. One day, his mother gave him one hundred coins and told him to buy a donkey at the market. Before he left, she warned him, "Be sure the donkey you buy is healthy, and don't let anyone take advantage of you."

The boy set off. On the way, he passed a farmer working in his fields. "Good day, young man. Where are you going?" asked the farmer.

"I'm on my way to the market," replied the boy. "My mother gave me one hundred coins to buy a donkey." Just at that moment, the boy noticed some watermelons growing in the farmer's field. He had never seen a watermelon before, so he asked the farmer, "What are those?"

"They're donkey eggs," said the farmer, who decided to play a trick on the foolish boy. "All you have to do is put one of these eggs in a warm place. Before long, a little donkey will hatch from it."

"Really?" asked the boy, whose eyes grew wide with excitement.

"Really," replied the farmer. "This is your lucky day. You can save yourself a trip to the market."

"How much do they cost?" asked the boy.

"For you, one donkey egg for one hundred coins."

The boy thought how lucky he was to have *just* that amount! He believed everything the farmer said. He forgot everything his mother said.

* Algeria is pronounced al-JEER-ee-ah. It is a country in northwestern Africa.

The boy quickly paid the farmer, picked out the biggest watermelon, and started back home. But as he walked, the watermelon began to feel heavy. When the boy got to the top of a steep hill, he put it down. Then he sat on the watermelon and rested for awhile. Soon he fell asleep. As he slept, he slid off the watermelon, and it began to roll down the hill.

The boy jumped up and chased after it. The watermelon hit a rock and split in half. It startled a rabbit sleeping nearby. When the boy saw the rabbit, he thought it was a baby donkey. "Look!" he cried. "My donkey already has long ears, and I'm sure its short tail will soon grow long.

"Run to my house, little donkey! Run to my house!" shouted the boy. The rabbit paid no attention. It scurried off in the other direction and was soon out of sight.

"You'd better listen to me!" yelled the boy as he ran off chasing the rabbit. "I'll catch you yet!"

Of course, he never did. And that noodlehead is probably still out there somewhere, chasing after his baby donkey.

About the story

This numskull story is found in many countries throughout the world including France, Russia, Ireland, the United States, and Turkey. Although sometimes it's told with a pumpkin rather than a watermelon and with a horse rather than a donkey, the idea is the same.

Tips for telling

When the mother warns the boy before he goes off to buy a donkey, look right at the audience and pretend you are the mother talking to the boy. Keep your eyes moving across the whole audience so that everyone feels involved. When the boy notices the watermelons, pretend to see them with your eyes.

Be sure to show that the boy doesn't think. Instead, he automatically believes everything the farmer says. For example, make your eyes grow wide and sound very excited and innocent when the boy says, "Really?" Then use a tricky voice and expression on your face when the man says, "Really." Make it clear to your listeners that the man is like a sly fox and that the boy really should know better than to trust him.

Such a Silly, Senseless Servant

A Story from China

An important Chinese judge had a very silly servant. Despite the fact that he was a numskull, the servant was kindhearted and well-meaning, and so the judge, who was very kind himself, could never bring himself to fire him.

One day, the judge heard that his servant had been arrested and put in jail. He hurried to ask him what he had done. "Oh, nothing much. I saw a rope lying on the ground and picked it up."

"What?" cried the judge. "Why would they punish you so harshly for picking up a piece of rope?"

"Well," replied the servant, "you see, I didn't notice that there was a cow on the other end of it."

The judge scratched his head and said to himself, "Such a silly, senseless servant!"

Another time, when the servant was working in the fields, the judge called for him to come inside. "I'll be right there," shouted the servant at the top of his lungs. "Just as soon as I hide my hoe over here in the last row."

When the servant went into the house, the judge scolded him. "You fool! You shouldn't yell so loudly for everyone to hear. Every thief in town will know where you've hidden your hoe!"

When the servant went back outside, sure enough, his hoe was gone. He returned to the house and *whispered* to the judge, "You're right. A thief has stolen my hoe."

The judge cried, "It's too late to whisper now. The hoe's already been stolen!" Then he rolled his eyes and said to himself, "Such a silly, senseless servant!"

One day, the judge was walking to a meeting with his servant at his side. The judge felt quite uncomfortable as he walked. He looked down and saw the problem right away. His boots didn't match. One had a thick sole, the other a thin one. He said to his servant, "My boots got mixed up this morning. Please take these home and bring back a good pair."

When the servant got back, he was empty-handed. "Where on earth are the boots I asked you to bring?" cried the judge.

"I have bad news for you," replied the servant. "The pair of boots at home were exactly the same as the ones you were wearing. One had a thick sole and one thin. They would be just as uncomfortable, so I didn't see any reason to bring them."

The judge tried to explain that he should have brought either two shoes with thick soles or two with thin soles. At last he threw up his hands and said to himself, "Such a silly, senseless servant!"

From then on, the judge tried to make his orders as clear and simple as possible. But in spite of his efforts, at least once a day his servant's foolishness would cause him to sigh and say to himself, "Such a silly, senseless servant!"

About the story

The last incident in this story brings to mind the old joke where one guy points out to his friend that he has on two different socks. The friend cleverly answers, "Do you like them? Why, I have another pair just like them at home in my drawer."

43

Tips for telling

Because of the repetition of the "s" sound, be sure to say "Such a silly, senseless servant!" very clearly so your listeners will easily understand you. You may wish to have the audience join in each time you say the phrase. If so, when you introduce the story, say something like, "This story is called 'Such a Silly, Senseless Servant!' That line, 'Such a silly, senseless servant!' will repeat again and again, and I'd like you to join in when I say it. At the count of three, let's all practice saying it together. One, two, three, 'Such a silly, senseless servant!' Each time I want you to join in, I'll motion to you."

Use body language to show the difference between the servant and the judge. You could, for example, hold your body in a tall, straight, serious manner for the judge and slump down a bit for the servant. Practice while looking into a mirror to see if you are clearly showing the difference between the two.

To make sure your listeners know the story is over, sound very frustrated when you say the final "Such a silly, senseless servant!" and then confidently take a bow.

No Doubt about It

A Story from Iran

A dishonest man owned a beautiful parrot that he taught to say, "No doubt about it!" He then buried some gold pieces in different places around his village. The next morning he went around town bragging, "My parrot is very wise. Just watch. He can even tell me where to dig for money."

Some of the townspeople were very interested. They watched as he said, "Oh, wise parrot, if I dig here, will I find any gold?"

"Brrrrk! No doubt about it!" was the parrot's reply. Of course, the man then dug up the money and showed it to everyone.

A young man, who was quite greedy and didn't like to work, watched the parrot's owner do this in a few different spots. He thought, "If I owned that parrot, I'd soon be rich." The parrot's owner offered to sell the parrot for fifty gold pieces. The young man was shocked. He said, "That's a lot of money!" The parrot's owner replied, "Oh, but sir, my parrot is well worth it. Isn't that true, oh wise one?"

"Brrrrk! No doubt about it!" said the parrot.

This answer pleased the foolish young man. He handed over the money and walked off with the parrot. He spent the rest of the afternoon searching for gold. But though he dug and dug wherever the parrot told him, he never found a single gold piece. At last he said to the parrot, "I guess *I* was the one who was tricked. What a fool I was to let my greed get the best of me. I've wasted fifty gold pieces."

"Brrrrk! No doubt about it!" was the parrot's reply.

"Well, at least you told me the truth once," said the young man as he laughed at his own foolishness. "I've learned my lesson. From now on, I'm going to work. That's the best way to make money."

And, of course, the parrot replied, "Brrrrk! No doubt about it!"

About the story

This story brings to mind the old saying, "A fool and his money are soon parted." Parrots are among the most intelligent birds. They can learn to solve somewhat complex problems, and many of them can be taught to talk. Because of this, there are numerous folktales such as this one in which parrots help make human beings look foolish.

Tips for telling

When the parrot speaks, your listeners will really enjoy the story if you use a squawky parrot voice. You could also pretend to flap your wings as the parrot speaks. (Fold your arms in close to your body and stick your elbows out to the side.) Use your voice and body language to show the young man's greed and, then later, his disappointment.

When Giufà Guarded the Goldsmith's Door

A Story from Italy

If ever there were a fool in this world, it was Giufà.* He lived in a small village in Italy long, long ago. Giufà always tried to do the right thing. Unfortunately, his idea of the right thing was so silly that it usually got him into trouble.

One day, Giufà got a job with a goldsmith. On his first day of work, the goldsmith told him, "Giufà, I am leaving now to do an errand. While I'm gone, you must guard the door."

"Yes, of course, sir," said Giufà. It was his first job and he wanted to please his boss. "I'll guard the door very carefully."

But later, when the goldsmith returned, there was no sign of Giufà or the door! His store was wide open and unattended. Just down the street a crowd of people had gathered to watch some actors put on a show. There stood Giufà in the crowd, holding the door on his back.

The goldsmith was furious. He ran over

*Giufà is pronounced JOO-fah.

and said, "Giufà, didn't I ask you to guard my store while I was gone? Instead, you've left it wide open. Why, thieves could have stolen everything!"

"But, sir," replied Giufà, "you never told me to guard the store. You told me to guard the door. Look, here it is, safe and sound. I've guarded it very carefully."

Needless to say, that was Giufà's first and last day on the job.

About the story

There's sometimes a fine line between the wise man and the fool. Giufà seems to be quite innocent and foolish in this story as we tell it. He follows directions in a very exact way but doesn't use common sense. However, the story could be interpreted and told differently. If you suspected that Giufà carried the door on purpose and really understood the foolishness of what he was doing, the meaning of the story would change. Perhaps he saw the actors down the road and came up with the whole idea so that he would have an excuse to leave the store and go see them.

Tips for telling

It's very important that you say, "Guard the *door*," when the goldsmith leaves to go on his errand. When he returns, be sure he asks, "Didn't I ask you to guard my *store*?" When the goldsmith speaks, show with your body and your voice that he is very angry that his store has been left wide open. When Giufà replies, change your body to show his carefree attitude.

The Men with Mixed-Up Feet

A Story from Russia

One summer day, seven silly men set off to the market to sell their sheep. They walked and walked, but it took longer than expected. The sun set before they arrived at the market, so they had to spend the night out under the stars. Since it was a chilly evening, they decided to lie on the ground in a line, each one right next to the other. But both of the men on the ends complained, "This isn't fair! The rest of you are in the middle! We're going to freeze here on the ends!"

The five men lying in the middle quickly thought of a solution. "Listen, you two just lie down between us." That was fine until the two men who were now on the ends got cold and started to protest. The noodleheads kept on changing positions. They didn't understand that no matter what they did, two of them would always be on the ends.

It would have been a long, cold, sleepless night if a farmer who lived nearby had not come along. He watched the men getting up, switching positions, and then lying down again. The farmer thought to himself, "Noodleheads, no doubt." He approached them and asked, "It looks as if you have a problem. May I help?"

After the fools explained their situation, the farmer said, "Don't worry. I know just what to do." He placed a small, round stone on the ground. "Each of you lie on the ground with your feet touching the stone."

When the seven silly men tried this, they were amazed. They were now lying in a circle with their feet at the center. Each man was between two other men. They all felt warm and cozy. The numskulls praised the farmer for his wisdom and quickly fell asleep. Seeing this, the farmer continued on his way.

When the fools woke up in the morning, they found that their feet had become tangled up during the night.

"Whose feet are whose?" one cried.

"How will we get up if we can't find our own feet?" shrieked another.

"Oh no, we're stuck here!" they wailed. The men grew hungry and thirsty, but still they sat there, thinking they couldn't get up. After a while, even their sheep grew frustrated. They giggled and rolled their eyes and began to wander away.

Just when the fools were beginning to think they'd be there forever, the same farmer passed by again. He was surprised to see the men lying on the ground, their feet all jumbled together. He approached them and asked, "What's the problem now?"

One of the fools replied, "Can't you see? Somehow during the night our feet got all mixed-up. We're stuck here until we sort out this terrible mess. Can you help us?"

The farmer didn't say a word. He just picked up a twig and began to tickle the bottoms of their feet. The men giggled and jumped to their

feet. To their amazement, they were all standing, each on his own pair of feet.

The men thanked the farmer, and he went on his way. Then the seven noodleheads gathered up their sheep and went on their way, thrilled to once again have their own feet back.

About the story

The problem of mixed-up feet is common in world folktales. We found similar stories told in Mexico, Poland, Turkey, Iceland, and Scotland. "The Mixed-Up Feet and the Silly Bridegroom," a Jewish/Polish story that includes this theme, can be found in one of our favorite books, *Zlateh the Goat and Other Stories*, by Isaac Bashevis Singer. Singer wrote a number of wonderful books about the fools of the village of Chelm, all of which we recommend.

Tips for telling

Use hand gestures to show how the men are lying right alongside one another. This will help your listeners get a clear picture of the scene in their minds. Later, when the farmer shows them how to form a circle, gesture to show the rock in the middle. Then, make a circular motion when you describe how they are all lying in a circle with their feet in the center.

When the silly men think that their feet have become entangled, sound extremely upset and desperate. When they jump to their feet after the farmer tickles them, make a jumping movement with your upper body. Gesture down toward your feet and show amazement when you say, "Now they were all standing, each on his own pair of feet."

Next Time I'll Know What to Do

A Story from England

Jack and his mother lived in a tiny house in a small village. They were quite poor, but because his mother worked so hard, they managed to get by. But Jack was lazy. *Very* lazy. On beautiful summer days he would lie by the creek and bask in the sun. When the winter came, he spent most of his time in front of the fireplace.

Finally, Jack's mother had had enough. One morning she said, "Jack, it's time for you to get a job!" Jack could tell from his mother's tone of voice that she meant business, so he set off to find a job. And he found one. All day long he worked in the fields for a farmer and received a coin for his payment. Jack was delighted. He had never had any money before. He couldn't wait to show his mother.

On the way home, he held the coin up and showed it to everyone he met. But as he crossed over a bridge, he dropped the coin into the water below. When he got home, his mother cried, "Oh, Jack, that's no way to carry money. Why didn't you put it in your pocket? Then you wouldn't have lost it!"

"*Ohhhhh!*" said Jack. "Next time I'll know what to do."

The next day Jack helped the farmer's wife churn butter. At the end of the day, Jack was given two slabs of butter. He wanted to please his mother, so he did just what she had told him. He put the butter in his pockets and started home. But soon the butter began to melt and drip down his pants. By the time Jack got home, he was a greasy mess.

"Oh, Jack," wailed his mother. "You weren't thinking. You should have wrapped the butter in wet leaves so it wouldn't melt and carried it carefully in your hands."

"*Ohhhhh!* Next time I'll know what to do."

The next day Jack worked for the baker and was rewarded with a large cat. Since they needed a good mouser, Jack knew his mother would be pleased. Again he did just as she had told him, but it wasn't easy. The cat screeched and scratched as he wrapped it in wet leaves. On the way home, it got one paw free and gave him a good scratch. Then it jumped to the ground and darted away.

When Jack got home, his mother said, "Oh, Jack! Do I have to tell you everything? The way to carry a cat is to tie a string around its neck and then pull it along behind you."

"*Ohhhhh!* Next time I'll know what to do."

The next day Jack worked for the butcher and was paid with a big slab of meat. Jack remembered his mother's advice. He tied the meat with a string and dragged it along after him. By the time Jack got home, the meat was ruined.

"Oh, Jack, what am I going to do with you?" cried his mother. "Look at this meat. It's covered with dirt. The way to carry meat is on your shoulder!"

"*Ohhhhh!* Next time I'll know what to do."

The next day Jack was lucky enough to find a job with the richest man in town. He was asked to clean the barn where the man kept his donkeys. It was a hard, smelly job. At the end of the day, the man was so pleased that he gave Jack one of his donkeys. Although he was a very strong young man, Jack was worried when he remembered what his mother had told him. He finally managed to lift the donkey up and put it on his shoulders. Then slowly, very slowly, he walked out of the barn.

It happened that the rich man had a daughter who had never laughed in her life. The rich man had offered two big sacks of gold to anyone who could make her laugh. As Jack came out of the barn with the donkey on his shoulders, the rich man's daughter burst out laughing.

Her father was delighted and had his servants give Jack two big sacks of gold. Jack was bewildered. He stood there with the heavy donkey on his shoulders, wondering how he could carry the two sacks of gold as well. At last, he put the donkey down so he could think better. Then he actually had an idea. He tied the sacks together, hung them over the back of the donkey, and climbed on.

Jack's mother was amazed when he came riding home with not only a donkey but also two sacks of gold! She couldn't believe the clever way Jack had brought them back home. She cried, "Jack, you really can think for yourself!"

From that time on, Jack and his mother were quite wealthy, and he even managed to use his brains—at least now and then.

About the story

This story about Jack is a good example of the problems caused when someone follows directions literally, without using his brains. Jack always does exactly what his mother tells him to do. The problem is that he follows the right directions at the wrong time.

We have been telling this story for over twenty years and have found that it's always a crowd-pleaser. Listeners love to anticipate how Jack will foolishly apply his mother's directions to the next situation.

Tips for telling

There are two main characters who often talk back and forth to one another in this story. Be sure that you hold your body one way for Jack and another for his mother. Jack should seem carefree and silly, while his mother should grow more and more frustrated with him throughout the story.

Each time Jack says, *"Ohhhhh! Next time I'll know what to do,"* stretch out the *"Ohhhhh!"* You may want to have your listeners join in on that part.

When Jack picks up the donkey and puts it on his shoulders, you may want to mime that part. Be sure to show great strain in your voice as well.

The Hunter of Java

A Story from Indonesia (Java)*

Ali bin Bavah** was an ordinary hunter. But in his own mind, which was full of dreams, he was an extraordinary one. One day, he came upon a deer sleeping in some tall grasses. He thought, "Who but I, Ali bin Bavah, could creep up so quietly that a deer would not wake up?"

Ali bin Bavah was so pleased with himself. He stood right beside the deer, took out a pouch of tobacco, and lit his pipe. He hung the pouch on the sleeping deer's antler. As Ali bin Bavah watched the smoke curl from his pipe, he began to daydream. "This deer will provide plenty of meat for my family," he thought. "I'll take the rest and sell it at the market. With the money, I'll buy a huge flock of ducks. Everyone in the village will know I'm rich when they see my ducks. If a traveler should pass through the village and ask, 'Who owns all these ducks?' the villagers will reply, 'Why, Ali bin Bavah, the greatest hunter in all of Java!'

"Next, I'll sell the ducks and buy a herd of goats. My neighbors will be amazed that one person could have so many goats. If anyone should ask, 'Who owns all these goats?' the villagers will reply, 'Why, Ali bin Bavah, the greatest hunter in all of Java!'

"Before long, I'll sell the goats and buy a herd of water buffalo. They'll give the tastiest milk around and do all the hard work in my fields. If anyone should ask, 'Who owns all these water buffalo?' the villagers will reply, 'Why, Ali bin Bavah, the greatest hunter in all of Java!'

*Indonesia is a country that consists of a group of islands in southeast Asia. It is pronounced In-doe-NEE-sha; Java, which is one of the islands, is pronounced JAHV-uh.

**Ali bin Bavah is pronounced AH-lee-behn-BAH-vah.

"When I'm tired of the water buffalo, I'll sell them and buy some elephants. Then *everyone* will know how important I am. If anyone should ask, 'Who owns all these elephants?' the villagers will reply, 'Why, Ali bin Bavah, the greatest hunter in all of Java!'

"The rajah* himself will hear of my elephants and ask to buy them. When I go to the rajah's palace, his daughter will fall madly in love with me. We'll marry and have twins. To show our children the world, we'll buy an enormous ship and sail the seas. When a small ship passes by and someone asks, 'Who owns this magnificent ship?' our servants will reply, 'Why, Ali bin Bavah, the greatest hunter in all of Java!'"

By now the young hunter was lost in his daydreams. He swayed back and forth with the movement of his imaginary ship. But then, in his mind's eye, he saw his children playing too close to the edge of the boat. He screamed, "Get back! You'll fall in!"

As Ali bin Bavah cried out, he woke the sleeping deer. Before he could throw his spear, the deer quickly bounded away with the tobacco pouch on its antlers. He called after the deer, "Come back, you thief! You've taken my wife, my children, all my riches…and my tobacco pouch!"

*A rajah is a prince or chief. Rajah is pronounced RAHJ-uh.

There was nothing that the young hunter could do. His royal life had vanished. He headed toward home. As he walked, he found his tobacco pouch lying on the ground where it had fallen from the deer's antlers. Undaunted, he smiled and thought to himself, "Who owns this tobacco pouch?" And then he answered, "Why, Ali bin Bavah, the greatest hunter in all of Java!"

About the story

The theme of lost dreams is often found in world folktales. The most well known story is an Aesop fable about a milkmaid who walks along daydreaming as she carries a pail of milk on her head. She thinks she will sell the milk and buy eggs that will hatch into chicks, which she will sell and buy a calf, then a horse, and so on. At the end, while lost in thought, she tosses her head to show that she will be so rich and snooty that she won't even speak to common people. The milk is spilled, and that's the end of her daydreams. From that story comes the common expression, "Don't count your chickens before they've hatched."

Tips for telling

To tell this story, you must pretend to be a braggart. Show how important Ali bin Bavah thinks he is by holding your shoulders high and speaking with authority. Grow more and more excited as his plans get bigger and bigger. At the end, show how disappointed he is when he awakens the deer and it runs off.

Listeners love to feel as if they're part of a story. The audience will enjoy joining in on the line, "Why, Ali bin Bavah, the greatest hunter in all of Java!" After you say this line the first time, say something like: "This line will be repeated over and over in the story. Would you join in and help me with it?" Then repeat the line and have them join in. The next time the line comes up in the story, motion toward your listeners to let them know it's time to participate.

Seven Foolish Fishermen

A Story from France

Long ago, in a small village in France, there lived seven brothers. They were known not only for their great skill as fishermen but also for their complete lack of sense.

One day they decided to take a trip to Paris. None of them had ever left his little village before. Their mother was worried. She warned them, "It's easy to get lost in such a big city. Be sure to watch out for each other."

It was a three-day walk to Paris, so they set out early. The brothers made good time as they talked of all the sights they would see. At midday, they came upon a large well. They took a drink, ate their lunch, and rested for awhile.

When it was time to continue on their way, the oldest brother remembered what his mother had said. He decided they had better count to make sure no one had gotten lost so far. He lined his brothers up and counted, "One, two, three, four, five, six. What? Only six? I must have counted wrong. Someone else try." But when the second oldest brother counted, he, too, came up with only six. All the brothers tried, and all got the same result. They didn't realize that each of them had forgotten to count himself.

"Oh, no!" they cried. "One of us is missing!" They began to call and look around for their lost brother. They looked up in the trees and behind the bushes, but he was nowhere to be found.

One of them happened to look over the edge of the well. When he saw his reflection in the water at the bottom, he thought it was his lost brother. He called to the others, "I've found him! He's fallen in the well, but he seems to be fine."

"Don't be scared," he called to his brother down in the well. "We'll have you out of there in no time."

The other brothers came running. They couldn't figure out how to rescue the lost brother without a rope or a ladder. Then the youngest had an idea. "I've got it," he said. "We must form a chain down into the well so that our brother can climb up and make his escape."

They agreed this was a brilliant idea. The eldest brother held on to the top of the well, and the next brother climbed down and got hold of his ankles. It wasn't long before the brothers hung from each other's ankles.

But just then, the oldest brother felt a big sneeze coming on. *"Ah-ah-ah-choo!"* When he sneezed, he let go of the top of the well and tumbled in along with all his brothers. Now they were stuck at the bottom of the well. At least, they reasoned, they were all together again.

The brothers noticed that there were gaps between the stones, just big enough so they could use their hands and feet to climb out. Before long, they were all out of the well. Since their clothes were dripping wet, they took them off and hung them in a tree to dry. When a stranger passed by and saw them all standing there wearing only their underwear, he asked them what had happened. They explained about losing their brother and rescuing him from the well. "Sir," said the oldest brother. "We'd like to be absolutely sure we're all here. Would you please count us?"

"I have a better idea," said the stranger, who was doing his best not to laugh. "Since you all hung your pants up to dry, why don't you count how many pairs of pants are hanging in the tree?"

The brothers knew a good idea when they heard one. They counted and were pleased to find there were *seven* pairs of pants! They thanked the stranger again and again for his cleverness.

When the clothes were dry, the brothers decided to go home. If one of them had almost gotten lost on the *way* to Paris, surely one of them would get lost *in* Paris. They returned home, thankful they were all safe and sound.

About the story

The idea of forgetting to count oneself is a theme common to world stories. Likewise, there are also many tales about seeing one's reflection and thinking it to be someone else. In one story from India, a jackal convinces a lion that a bigger, more ferocious lion lives down in a well. The lion growls and threatens his reflection. He finally grows so angry that he jumps into the well and drowns.

Tips for telling

When you have opposing thoughts or ideas in a story, it's often effective to gesture to one side and then to the other. For example, at the beginning, when you describe their "great skill as fishermen," make a hand movement to your left and have an appropriate expression on your face. Then gesture toward the right when you speak of their "complete lack of sense."

When the oldest brother counts, pretend to count six *imaginary* brothers. Face the audience as you do this but don't actually look at your listeners and count them, or you may start giggling or get distracted. Look very puzzled when you don't see a seventh brother.

When one brother looks down into the well and thinks he sees his brother, pretend to look down into a well and get very excited. Use hand motions to show the chain the brothers make down into the well.

The King Brought Down by One Blow

A Story from the Philippines*

Long ago in the Philippines, there lived a powerful king. Unfortunately, he was also quite foolish. One day he announced, "It is now against the law for anyone to speak too loudly. Whoever raises his voice will be thrown into jail!"

The people went around whispering to each other. But even this didn't satisfy the king because now the animals sounded too loud. So the next day he declared, "From now on, it is against the law for animals to make too much noise!"

As you might imagine, this didn't work very well. Right after the king's announcement, one of his officers heard Frog croak. The officer caught Frog and brought him to be tried before the king.

The king began the trial by asking, "Don't you know there is a law that forbids animals to make too much noise?"

Frog replied, "Yes, your majesty. But I couldn't help laughing when I saw Snail carrying his house on his back wherever he goes."

Then the king called for Snail and asked, "Why do you always carry your house with you?"

"Your majesty, it's quite simple. If I don't, I'm afraid Firefly will set it on fire."

Next the king ordered Firefly to appear before him. "Why do you always carry fire with you? Don't you know it frightens other animals?"

"I know, your majesty. But if I don't carry it with me, Mosquito will bite me."

*Philippines is pronounced FILL-ih-peens.

Without delay, Mosquito was called. The king asked, "Why are you always trying to bite someone? Don't you know what a pest you are?"

"But, your majesty, I can't live unless I bite someone!"

By now, the king was tired of the trial, and he decided to put an end to it. He said to Mosquito, "I forbid you to bite anyone! From now on, it will be against the law for mosquitoes to bite!"

Mosquito tried to protest. "But your majesty, that's impossible!"

The king didn't want to be bothered by Mosquito's talk. He picked up a large stick to crush Mosquito.

Seeing this, Mosquito flew up and landed right on the king's nose. This made the king so angry that he smashed Mosquito with his stick.

That was the end of poor Mosquito. But at the same time, the king knocked himself out and fell to the ground.

There's no way to be sure whether or not that blow knocked any sense into the foolish king. But one thing is certain, there are plenty of other mosquitoes still biting people to this day.

About the story

The end of this story is similar to one told about the Italian fool, Giufà, who complains to a judge about being bothered by flies. When the judge says there's nothing he can do, Giufà argues that the judge is the one who is supposed to punish those who bother others. The judge laughs and gives Giufà permission to strike a fly wherever he sees one. Just then a fly lights on the judge's nose, and foolish Giufà makes a fist and smashes the judge's nose. For another story about Giufà, see "When Giufà Guarded the Goldsmith's Door" on page 47.

Tips for telling

When you speak as the king, hold your shoulders high and look as regal as possible. Practice while looking in a mirror. Speak loudly and forcefully. In contrast, when you speak as each one of the animals, hunch down a bit to show that it is frightened by the king's power.

Clever Elsie

A Story from Germany

In a little village in Germany, long ago, there lived a young woman named Elsie who was *always* thinking. Unfortunately, her thoughts were ridiculous. Elsie worried about *everything*. If she swallowed a cherry pit, she was sure a tree would soon be growing out of her head. If a dog barked at her, she worried that she couldn't understand what it was saying, since it might be trying to tell her something important. And when she sneezed a *big* sneeze, "AH, AH, CHOO!" she was afraid she might blow her family out the door.

The other villagers, who were fools themselves, thought Elsie must be very wise. They said, "Why, no one else ever thinks of the things she does!" And so they called her Clever Elsie.

A young man named Hans heard about Elsie. He thought, "If she is as clever as they say, I'd like to meet her. Why, if she is truly *that* clever, I'd like to marry her."

One day Hans found the courage to knock on her door. Elsie's parents welcomed Hans and invited him to stay for dinner. As they sat down at the table, Elsie's father said, "Elsie, please go to the cellar and bring us some cider."

Elsie, who had already taken a liking to Hans, grabbed a jug and hurried down to the cellar. She turned the tap on the cider barrel and began to fill the jug. Just then, she looked up and saw an ax hanging above her head. As usual, Elsie's mind began to work overtime. She thought, "If Hans and I get married, we'll have a baby. And when the baby grows up and we send him down here to fetch some cider, that ax might fall and kill him!" Elsie sat down and began to cry while the cider kept running all over the floor.

When Elsie didn't return after awhile, her mother went to the cellar and found her crying. When she asked what was the matter, Elsie replied, "If Hans and I get married, we'll have a baby. And when the baby grows up and we send him down here to fetch some cider, that ax might fall and kill him!" Her mother said, "Elsie, you are a clever one to think of such things!" Then the mother sat down on the bench beside Elsie and began to cry, too.

By this time the father was growing impatient. He went to the cellar and found his wife and daughter weeping and cider spilling all over the floor. He asked, "What on earth are you two crying about?"

"Why shouldn't we cry?" wailed Elsie. "If Hans and I get married, we'll have a baby. And when the baby grows up and we send him down here to fetch some cider, that ax might fall and kill him!"

"Now that's thinking ahead!" said her father proudly. Then he, too, sat down on the bench and began to cry.

Hans was now sitting all by himself at the supper table. He decided he had better see what had happened to everyone. In the cellar he found the three of them bawling their eyes out and cider spilt all over the floor.

First, Hans turned off the tap on the cider. Then, he calmed them down and asked what the problem was. Elsie explained, "Hans, if you and I get married, we'll have a baby. And when the baby grows up and we send him down here to fetch some cider, that ax might fall and kill him!"

Hans was amazed. He replied, "Elsie, I have never met anyone who can think the way you do! You're clever enough for both of us. Will you marry me?"

Elsie didn't have to think hard about that. They were married and lived quite happily together. Hans and Elsie had several children who often went to the cellar to draw cider. They always returned unharmed, and to this day, that ax hangs safely in the cellar.

About the story

Those of us who are worrywarts will see ourselves in Elsie, even though she is certainly an extreme example. We can spend a lot of wasted time worrying about something that never happens and then feel like a real noodlehead afterward. Worrying is only useful when it helps identify something we can do to prevent a bad thing from happening. Elsie could have simply taken the ax down and solved the problem immediately.

In some versions of this story, the young man who comes to court her is so amazed at her silliness that he decides to go off and find three other people as silly as Elsie.

Tips for telling

Each time Elsie worries about the ax falling on her child, look and sound very upset. A few sniffles and cries throughout her speech will add to the effect. Right after she says, "The ax might fall and kill him," let out a good "Boo hoo hoo!" It's very important that people are able to understand what you're saying, so make sure you speak clearly when Elsie cries as she talks. When someone comes down to ask her why she's crying, be sure to sound baffled and have a look of confusion on your face.

The Man Who Didn't Know
What *Minu** Meant
*A Story from Ghana***

Long ago, a poor man lived in a small village in Ghana. He owned a tiny hut and had few possessions. One day, he had to travel to a large city on the coast of Ghana. His neighbors warned him that people on the coast spoke a different language. They encouraged him to find someone to help him understand that language. But since he always thought he knew best, he paid no attention. "What do my neighbors know?" he said to himself. "Surely I'll be able to communicate with the people somehow."

As he neared the city, he came upon a great herd of cows. He thought, "My goodness, such a herd must belong to a very wealthy man. If only *I* owned such a herd!" He stopped the herder and asked, "Who owns all of these cows?" Since the herder didn't know the poor man's language, he replied, "Minu," which meant, "I don't understand," in his own language.

The foolish man assumed that Minu was the name of the owner of the cows. He thought he understood the herder perfectly. He said to himself, "My neighbors were wrong. I'll have no trouble communicating with the people here."

He kept walking until he came to the main street of the city, where he was amazed by the sights. He stopped to stare at a magnificent building and thought, "If only *I* owned such a building!" He asked a passerby who the owner was. Since the passerby didn't understand him, he also answered, "Minu." The poor man thought, "So, Mr. Minu owns property as well as animals."

*Minu is pronounced mih-NOO. In the Ga language of Ghana it means "I don't understand."

**Ghana, a country in West Africa, is pronounced GAH-na.

A little further down the street, he came to a bustling market. People were selling all sorts of things he had never seen or even heard of in his small village. He thought, "If only *I* owned all these things!" He asked a woman, "Where do all these things come from?" Not understanding him, she answered, "Minu." The poor man thought, "Minu owns this, Minu owns that, Minu owns everything!"

At last the poor man arrived at the harbor. There he watched dozens of men unloading a splendid ship. He thought, "If only *I* owned such a ship!" He asked another onlooker, "Who owns this extraordinary vessel?" Of course, the man answered, "Minu."

The poor man was astounded. "Why, Mr. Minu must be the wealthiest man in all of Ghana!"

After taking care of his business, he set out for home. Just as he was leaving the city, he came upon a funeral procession. When he asked one of the mourners the name of the dead person, he received the usual answer, "Minu."

The poor man found this hard to believe. He thought, "It's sad that Mr. Minu, in spite of all his riches, had to die like any common man. His wealth couldn't keep him from the grave. In the end, we're all the same. From now on, I'll be more content with my small hut and few possessions."

Even though the foolish man never realized that he hadn't understood a word that had been spoken in the city, at least he had learned an important lesson.

About the story

The man in this story is a noodlehead because he makes assumptions—he thinks he knows everything. This story reminds us that it's especially important not to make assumptions while we're visiting a foreign place! The man is also foolish because he doesn't listen when everyone tells him to learn a bit of the people's language. Just knowing a few words would have solved the problem.

Tips for telling

Don't forget to say that "Minu" means "I don't understand," or the story won't make any sense to your listeners. Each time the poor man asks who owns something, be sure to convey amazement. Remember that he lives in a small village and has never seen large buildings or ships. When the people reply, "Minu," look confused and say it as you imagine someone might say, "I don't understand." But at the same time, remember that the poor man thinks they're saying a person's name. The confused look on the people's faces makes him think they're saying, "Why, who else but Minu, of course?" Practice in a mirror until you feel that your reply could be interpreted either way.

The Fool's Feather Pillow

A Story from Ireland

Long ago in Ireland, there lived a fool who wished to seek his fortune in Dublin. One day, he set off toward the big city. As he walked, he happened to pass a dead goose lying on the side of the road.

Even though the numskull didn't know much about city life, he had heard that city people were so rich they slept on pillows stuffed with goose feathers. The people in his village could never afford such a luxury. They slept on pillows stuffed with hay or straw.

The fool was eager to try a fancy goose pillow. He thought, "I won't have to wait till I get to Dublin. I'll try it out right now." So he pulled out one of the goose's feathers and put it on the hard ground. Then he lay down and put his head on the feather.

"This feather isn't very comfortable," he thought. He twisted and turned as he tried to rest, but he couldn't get in a good position. His head hurt. His face ached. After lying there for a while, he couldn't stand it any longer.

"If sleeping on *one* feather is so very uncomfortable," thought the fool, "I don't know how anyone could stand to sleep on a *whole* pillow full of them! The people of Dublin must not be very wise. I have no desire to visit a city of fools." He got up and headed back to his own village.

When the noodlehead returned home, he was tired from all the walking. He lay down and happily fell fast asleep thinking there was nothing better than his own straw pillow.

About the story

The fool in this story doesn't have a bit of common sense. Common sense is the everyday, ordinary kind of information we all need to get by. Instead of coming to the logical conclusion that it would take a lot of feathers to make a comfortable pillow, he assumes that a whole bunch of feathers would be even more uncomfortable than one!

Tips for telling

Use gestures to show how the fool pulls out a feather and puts it on the ground and then tries to get comfortable. Sound and look very confused when he says, "If sleeping on *one* feather is so uncomfortable, I don't know how anyone could stand to sleep on a *whole* pillow full of them!"

The Ninny Who Didn't Know Himself

A Story from Moldova*

Once a young farmer decided to visit his relatives who lived a good distance away. He set off on the two-day walk to their village. At the end of the first day, tired and hungry, he stopped at an inn. When he asked for a room, the innkeeper replied, "I have only one bed left. You're welcome to stay, as long as you don't mind sharing a room."

"Not at all," replied the farmer. "Please wake me before sunrise so I can get an early start. I'm anxious to see my cousins."

The farmer found that he was sharing the room with a priest. They talked a bit and soon fell fast asleep.

The next morning, when the innkeeper woke the farmer, it was still dark. The farmer dressed quickly and was soon on his way. After awhile, he stopped to rest under a tree. When he glanced down at himself, he saw he was wearing the priest's robes. He didn't realize he had put them on by mistake. Instead, he thought *he* must be the priest.

"Oh, *no!*" he cried. "That foolish innkeeper woke the priest by mistake! Now I'll have to go back to the inn to wake myself. At this rate, I'll never get to see my cousins."

He was furious that the innkeeper had been so careless. As he walked back, he kept calling the innkeeper names. "Ninny! Nitwit! Numskull!"

Anyone else would have known who the *real* fool was.

About the story

This theme of a person not knowing himself is common in world folklore. For example, in a version from Iran, a young man, who has lived all his life in the forests, visits a big city for the first time. When

*Moldova is pronounced mal-DOE-vah. It gained its independence from the Soviet Union in 1991.

he sees the huge crowds of people milling about, he wonders how he will ever know who he is among so many people. He ties a pumpkin to his leg so he will be different. While the young man is asleep, another fellow, who wishes to fool him, takes the pumpkin and ties it to his own leg. The young man wakes up thinking that the other man with the pumpkin on his leg must be him!

Tips for telling

When the farmer glances down at his clothes, look down at your own clothes. Your expression must first be of great surprise and alarm and then should quickly change to anger as he blames the innkeeper for waking the wrong man.

Deliver the last line slowly and with lots of feeling. Then take a bow so it's clear to your listeners that the story is over.

The Mayor's Golden Shoes

A Jewish Tale from Poland

Every village has its fools. But when it came to fools, the village of Chelm* in Poland struck gold. When you walked down the street, everyone you met, from the richest to the poorest, was a complete numskull.

When there was a problem, the townspeople went to the village elders, who were the oldest and biggest fools. They would be sure to come up with a complicated solution to a simple problem. Here's one of the many stories about the noodleheads of Chelm.

The mayor of Chelm had grown disgruntled. When he walked down the streets of the town, no one seemed to notice. At last he realized it was because he dressed just like everyone else. "Why would the villagers notice me?" he thought. "After all, I look no different than the butcher, the baker, or the tailor."

He spoke with the village elders, who were deeply troubled to see their mayor so upset. They thought long and hard. They pulled on their gray beards. They furrowed their brows and looked toward the skies for inspiration. Finally the eldest of the elders said, "I've got it! We'll have a pair of golden shoes made for the mayor. Wherever he goes, people will be sure to notice him."

When the golden shoes were ready, the mayor proudly put them on and walked down the street. But there had been a heavy rain, and the street was full of mud. As the mayor strolled along, his head held high, he realized that no one noticed him. He looked down and saw the reason. His golden shoes were covered with mud! The mayor returned to the elders to complain.

The elders thought long and hard. They pulled on their gray beards. They furrowed their brows and looked toward the skies for inspiration. Finally, the eldest of the elders said, "I've got it! We'll have a pair of fine

*Chelm is pronounced HELM.

leather shoes made to wear *over* the golden shoes. That way the golden shoes won't get muddy."

The mayor was delighted with this solution. Swollen with pride, he strutted down the street. But since not one glimmer of gold shone through the leather shoes, none of the villagers noticed him.

Again, he returned to the elders. They thought long and hard. They pulled on their gray beards. They furrowed their brows and looked toward the skies for inspiration. Finally the eldest of the elders said, "I've got it! All we have to do is put holes in the leather shoes so that the gold will shine through."

But when the mayor returned to the streets, it didn't take long for the mud to ooze into the holes. The golden shoes inside the leather ones were soon covered with mud. The mayor was irate. He returned to the elders and said, "I have never been so humiliated. I walk down the streets and people think I'm a beggar with my muddy shoes full of holes. No one knows how important I am. I quit!"

The elders pleaded with him to reconsider. They promised to come up with the perfect solution. The mayor agreed to give them one more chance.

The elders thought long and hard. They pulled on their gray beards. They furrowed their brows and looked toward the skies for inspiration. Finally the eldest of the elders said, "I've got it! He must wear his regular shoes on his feet and the golden shoes on his *hands*. That way, everyone will recognize him."

And it was true. Although the mayor's arms ached at the end of the day, and he could no longer shake hands or open doors, he proudly walked down the street with the golden shoes on his hands. And wherever he went, people were sure to notice him. The elders of Chelm had once again solved a problem as only *they* could.

About the story

Although many leaders are honest and hard-working, the people in power sometimes appear to be very foolish. Many cultures tell stories in which the flaws of leaders are made obvious. Although at first glance this seems to be a silly story, it was definitely told to make a point. The mayor is more concerned about whether everyone notices him than he is about doing his job, and the elders spend a lot of time thinking and yet come up with totally ridiculous solutions.

Tips for telling

The repetition in this story will make it easier to learn than you might expect. Each time the elders try to figure out a solution to the mayor's complaints, be sure to pretend to pull on your beard, furrow your brow, and look upward for inspiration. Have a look of great excitement when the eldest of the elders finally says, "I've got it!"

Use body language to show how unhappy the mayor is at the beginning and how proudly he walks down the street wearing the golden shoes at the end.

I'd Laugh, Too, If I Weren't Dead

A Story from Iceland

Once there were two women who got into an argument about whose husband was the greatest fool. When they couldn't settle the quarrel, they decided to put their husbands to the test. Each one vowed she would prove to the other that *her* husband was the biggest noodlehead.

The first woman immediately came up with a plan to make her husband look as foolish as possible. When he got home that evening, she was working at her sewing table. He watched as she went through all the motions of measuring and cutting—but without using any material. At last he was so puzzled that he couldn't help asking, "What are you doing?"

She replied, "I was hoping you wouldn't ask. You see, I've almost completed a brand new suit for you. I was planning to surprise you."

"But I don't see a thing," he replied.

"Of course you can't see it. It's the *very* finest material."

She went on and on about the suit until her husband began to believe that maybe he *could* see it. When he came home from the fields for lunch, she said, "Your brand new suit's ready." Then she pretended to help him try it on. She carefully smoothed out every wrinkle and oohed and aahed over the way he looked.

Her husband went along with this until at last he said, "This suit doesn't feel very warm."

"Well, of course not," replied his wife. "That's because it's so fine. You wouldn't expect it to feel as thick as the work clothes you wear every day. My, you look handsome. I can't wait till you get a chance to wear it." Even though the husband was only wearing his underwear, he was convinced that he had on a magnificent suit.

In the meantime, the other woman cooked up her plan. Before her husband got out of bed in the morning, she stared at him with great concern. "Look at you!" she said. "You're awfully pale. Don't get up, whatever you do. You're in no shape to go to the fields to work today."

Her husband, who felt quite fine, liked the idea of resting at home in bed for the day. He rolled over and went back to sleep. When he woke up, his wife had a look of shock and horror on her face. She cried, "Oh my goodness, you've taken a turn for the worse!" She brought in all kinds of medicine and herbs and began to doctor him. She was so convincing that her husband actually started to feel ill. She continued to fuss over him until the next day when the coffin that she had ordered arrived.

"What's this?" cried the husband.

"Why, it's a coffin," replied his wife. "Don't you know you're dead? You died in your sleep last night. Now, be quiet. Dead people don't talk."

By this time, the husband was so confused that he didn't know what to think. He figured his wife must be right. She usually was. So he lay down, closed his eyes, and didn't say another word. He was then placed in the coffin, which had air holes for him to breathe and a small window for him to see through.

The other villagers were told of the funeral. Soon, the mourners began to arrive. Before long, the other woman and her husband came. He was, of course, wearing his fine new suit. In spite of the sad occasion, everyone burst out laughing when they saw the fool in his underwear. The laughter was so loud that the man in the coffin opened his eyes and glanced out. When he saw the sight, he sat straight up in the coffin and shouted, "Why, I'd laugh, too…if I weren't dead!" Hearing this, the mourners laughed even louder.

In the end, the two women had to agree that it was a tie. Between *their* two husbands, there certainly was no telling who was the biggest noodlehead!

About the story

This tale is told throughout Europe, the Far East, and the Middle East. A wonderful version from the Southern Appalachian Mountains of the United States, "The Two Old Women's Bet," can be found in *Grandfather Tales* by Richard Chase (Boston: Houghton Mifflin, 1948).

The theme of a naked person (or one wearing only his underwear) being convinced that he's wearing clothes existed in folktales long before Hans Christian Andersen wrote "The Emperor's New Clothes." Be sure to compare this story to "Dead or Alive?" on page 20. Although both stories contain the idea that someone could actually convince another person that he's dead, the plots are quite different.

Tips for telling

The two women must sound very persuasive as they try to fool their husbands. When the first woman tries the new suit on her husband, pretend to look very pleased at how it looks on him. The second wife should look horrified as she tries to convince her husband that he's sick. Sound especially upset when she tells her husband he's dead.

When the "dead" man sits bolt upright in the coffin, make a movement with your head and upper body to suggest this. As he shouts, "Why, I'd laugh, too," look and sound as if you're laughing. Then pause, make your arms and body stiff, and change to a serious look on your face before you say, "if I weren't dead!"

General Tips for Telling Stories

As we mentioned in the introduction, you will find that the stories in this book are great fun to read aloud. They are folktales—stories passed down by word of mouth from one generation to the next. In many cases, they were told for hundreds of years before being written down. These stories are meant to be *heard*, and they will have the most impact when they are shared just as they used to be—told from memory, without a book, by one person to another.

If you're reading this section, it's probably because you have seen someone tell stories. Perhaps you were amazed by how captivating it can be to hear a person tell a story without props, costumes, or any special effects. Storytelling is as old as the world, and yet, even in our age of television, movies, and computer games, it can be a powerful experience. As a story is told, listeners see pictures in their minds. These pictures differ as people use their own imaginations, making storytelling a very personal experience. It is also a bonding time because there is always a sense that the audience has shared the same adventure.

You may be thinking, "It sounds like a lot of work to learn a story to tell. I'll bet it will be as good if I read it out loud." Not really. Just pick the story you enjoyed most and try telling it. You will find there is a big difference between reading a story to someone and telling it without the book. Without a text in hand, the storyteller is free to use facial expressions and body movements to make the telling more interesting. Your listeners will show much better attention and enjoyment of the story when you lay the book aside and put your heart into the story. As they listen to your words and watch your expression and movement, the story will spring to life for them.

If you would like to give storytelling a try, here are a few tips to get you started.

CHOOSING A STORY

Pick a story you *really* enjoy.

Although all the stories in this book are good for telling, you must be sure to choose one that really appeals to *you*. Your enthusiasm for the story is very important. When you love a story, your listeners sense your excitement and are swept along by your telling. If the storyteller sees and feels the places, characters, and events in the story, the listeners will as well.

If you have never told a story before, be sure to pick a short, simple one for your first telling. Once you are successful and see how much fun it can be, you can move on to more complicated stories. The more stories you tell, the more you'll discover what your strengths are. You may find that you're terrific at telling a nature myth or ghost story or that you're especially good at making people laugh. Perhaps you're good at all of them!

Consider who your audience will be.

Before you choose a story, think about the listeners. For your first experience, it may be easiest to tell stories to children. If they are very young, you must pick a story appropriate for them. Forget about those scary stories you love; save them for your peers. Some little ones frighten easily. Also be aware that young children may not understand the sophisticated humor of some of the stories in this book. Look for stories that are simple and straightforward. Young children love stories with a lot of repetition, and you can encourage them to join in on repeated phrases.

If you plan to tell the story for listeners your own age, the process of choosing is much easier. If you pick a story that you enjoy, more than likely your friends will enjoy it also.

LEARNING A STORY

Find a way of learning the story that works for you.

Many find it helpful to begin by doing a storyboard or cartoon drawing of the story. Sketch simple stick figures and scenes from the story, placing them in boxes, one after the other, to represent the tale's main events. The point is to help you learn the story, not to produce a work of art. If you prefer, you can make a written outline instead.

Next, try telling the story using your storyboard or outline. Begin by telling the story to yourself. Whenever possible, tell it out loud. Once you feel you know the story, put aside the storyboard or outline. This will help you get beyond simply memorizing to making the story your own. Go back and look at the original tale now and then to be sure you're not leaving out any important events or clever wordings.

Some tellers also find it very helpful to tell or read the story into a tape recorder and then listen to it until they feel they know it.

Tell the story again and again.

As soon as you're sure you remember the basic plot, tell it to someone else the first chance you get. Tell it to a friend while you're riding the school bus or to your family during dinner. Telling over and over helps you find what makes a story work—the details, voices, and expressions that bring it alive. Ask your listeners for suggestions. If they say that they had a hard time telling the difference between characters or that you spoke too quickly, you'll know what to work on. The more people you try it out on, the better, because every listener will notice different things.

It's also very helpful to practice in front of a mirror and to try out movements and facial expressions that will enhance the story.

Make the story your own.

Remember that the stories in this book represent other cultures. We encourage you to tell them in your own way, but you can't just change them around as you please and say they still represent a certain culture. When you first find a story you think you'd like to tell, make sure you feel comfortable with every part of it. If there's something that seems silly to you, you must ask yourself: can I change this part of the story in a way that won't harm the meaning? If the answer is "no," it's best to find a different tale to tell.

It's also wise to visit the library and read some background on the customs and ways of the people whose story you've chosen. You may learn interesting details that you could share with listeners in your introduction to the tale. But even if you don't mention what you've learned, you will do a better job of telling because you understand something about the original tellers.

Be sure to see the map on page 10 that shows where the people who told the stories in this book come from.

TELLING A STORY

To learn to be a good teller, watch other storytellers whenever you get the chance.

The best way to learn to tell stories is to observe as many storytellers as possible. Begin by paying close attention to friends, family members, classmates, teachers, or characters in a movie or television show. We are all storytellers, and some folks seem to come by their talents naturally. Carefully watch the people you love to listen to. Listen to their voices, watch their facial expressions, and observe their body movements. What is it they do that keeps your interest?

Try to observe some professional storytellers, if possible. These are people who get a lot of practice telling stories because they do it for a living. There are *many* different styles of telling. Watching a variety of storytellers will help you to see the possibilities and find a style you feel comfortable with. If you can't see a storyteller's performance in person, ask if your local library owns any videos of professional tellers.

Take your time—but don't go on *too* long!

When you tell your story, remember that you have the floor! The feeling that you are standing in front of a group of people with all eyes on you is both scary and very exciting. The adrenaline or extra energy that people often feel in this situation makes some tellers rush through a story. You can't really do justice to a tale if you speak too quickly. Listeners should be able to relax and enjoy a story, which is tough to do if the teller is talking a mile a minute. Slow down. Take your time.

On the other hand, don't dawdle, and never make the story longer than it needs to be. Take your cues from your listeners. This is good advice for everyday communication in general. You want listeners to look bright-eyed and interested. If they start to seem bored, you'll know you're going on too long and need to wrap it up.

Be expressive!

Although there are many important tips to keep in mind as you tell a story, the most important is to put expression or feeling in your voice, on your face, and in your body movements. If you are telling "Juan Bobo and the Pot That Would Not Walk," for example, you must let your listeners know just how furious Juan Bobo is when the pot does not move. Sound angry, have an angry look on your face, and also show the anger in your body. If you are telling "The King Brought Down By One Blow," you must really show a difference between the king and each of the animals brought before him. Nothing will bore an audience faster than a story told without expression.

Vary your voice!

There are many ways to change your voice. For example, although you must always speak loudly and clearly enough for everyone to hear, you would probably speak in a quieter voice when a character is scared or embarrassed. On the other hand, you might get loud when a character is angry or excited.

You should also vary the pitch of your voice. A low, deep pitch would be appropriate for a big bully or a monster. A higher pitch might be used for a tiny creature such as a mouse. Most characters would speak in a higher-pitched voice when they are excited or frightened. For example, think about how your voice might sound if you screamed "Help!"

Changing the speed or tempo of your voice can help create different moods and make the story interesting. If one character is chasing another, you would want to show the excitement by speaking more quickly during that part. On the other hand, to build suspense, speak slowly.

Don't be afraid of silence.

Every second of your story should *not* be filled with sound. Some of the most effective times in a story are when the teller pauses and there is complete silence. If, for example, a character opens the lid of a trunk filled with gold, pause and pretend to see the box's contents before you tell the listeners what's inside. Be sure to show the appropriate expression on your face in response to the gold.

Use a distinct character voice when necessary.

You will find that some characters in your story need special voices. If you choose to tell "No Doubt about It," it's very important that you feel comfortable imitating a parrot voice. The story just won't work without it.

As you are learning your story, think about your characters. If you are telling "Scissors," walk around the room the way you think the stubborn woman would walk. Hold your shoulders high and look as disagreeable as possible. Then try some voices until you find the way you think the woman would talk. Letting your body feel like the character will help you to find a good voice. When you've figured out the woman's voice, use the same process for her husband.

Use sound effects when appropriate.

Stories tend to be full of lots of interesting noises—doors creaking, wind blowing, babies crying. If you are good at imitating, such sounds can sometimes be used to enhance a story.

Use gestures and body movements to help listeners see pictures in their minds.

Gestures and body movements can help a story come alive. But any movements you make must help listeners see pictures in their minds. Simple movements, mostly from your waist up, will help your audience make visual images. If you get carried away and do too much movement, they will see only you and may lose the thread of the story. Take, for example, this action-packed sentence: "She hit the ball, ran to first, and slid into second." If you took a big, exaggerated swing, ran across the room, and then slid on the floor, you most likely would get a laugh. However, your listeners probably would have forgotten about the story. Remember, you're not in a play. Instead of really acting out the scene, stand in one place, facing the audience. As you say "hit," take a controlled swing and then run in place as you say "ran." As you say "slid," use one hand to make a quick sliding motion out toward the audience. The listeners will be able to see your face well and will be able to picture the busy scene clearly in their heads.

Look at your listeners.

It is very important that you maintain eye contact with your listeners throughout the story. A storyteller who looks down at the floor or above the heads of the audience will find it hard to keep people's attention. When one character speaks to another, make the listeners be the other character. For example, in "Next Time I'll Know What to Do" when Jack's mother says, "Jack, it's time for you to get a job!" look right at the audience as if you are Jack's mother and they are Jack.

It is sometimes very effective to pretend to "see" a person or an object as you tell the story. For example, when telling "The Man Who Didn't Know What *Minu* Meant," pretend to see a large herd of cows as you ask, "Who owns all these cows?" If you convince your listeners that you see the cows with your eyes, they will picture them as well.

Put expression on your face!

A good way to find out if you are putting the right expression on your face is to practice in a mirror. If a character is angry, you shouldn't be smiling.

One of the hardest challenges for many tellers is not to laugh at themselves when they tell in front of a group. For example, if a teller uses a terrific scared expression and the audience responds by laughing, the teller sometimes laughs, too. Remember to stay right in the story and keep looking scared. It's the listeners' job to laugh, not yours.

Try to include audience participation whenever appropriate.

Younger children love repetition. If a phrase is repeated again and again in a story, have them join in. After you say the phrase the first time, ask your listeners, "Why don't you do that with me?" Then do it again immediately so they can practice. When it comes around the next time, motion to them so they'll remember to join in.

Use your nervous energy to make the story better.

Being nervous is a sign that you have extra energy. Contrary to what you might think, this is good. Any performer or athlete needs extra energy. What's important is to use it in a positive way to improve your telling. The more energy you add, the better your storytelling will be.

There are two things you can do to help deal with nervousness. The first is to be well prepared. The more you practice, the more confident you will feel. It's a lot like taking a test in school. If you have studied the material, you know you will do your best. The second thing is to just do it! Your most difficult telling will be your first. Every time you face a group of listeners, it will feel a little easier. You will know the story better and be able to anticipate the listeners' reactions. Then you can really start to have fun with your story.

As one of our young storytellers said, "I thought I would be terrible at storytelling. But after I told my story, I felt great. I realized I could do something I never thought I could do. I won't be so afraid to try new things from now on."

Pass these stories on!

Tell the stories in this book whenever you get a chance. You could tell them at the dinner table to entertain your family or during a long car ride while on summer vacation. You also could tell them in front of your classmates at school. If you have to do an oral report on a country and would like to make it more interesting for the class, try telling a story as part of it. If you baby-sit for younger children, you will find there's no better way of entertaining them than telling stories. If you go camping or have a sleep-over with friends or a family reunion, those are also perfect times for telling tales.

So take the risk! Try telling a story, whether it's to a friend sitting on your front porch or to your whole class at school. As one ten-year-old storyteller said, "What matters most is having fun. You lighten everyone up by telling a story."

Follow-Up Activities

1. After you've read or told these stories, make up your own noodle-head stories. Here are some ideas to get you started:

   • Create your own noodlehead character and then make up stories about him or her. Think about how she/he would do everyday, ordinary things such as shopping for food at the supermarket, playing a sport, or going to school.

   • Take a character from this book, such as Clever Elsie, and make up more stories about her adventures.

   • Take two or three of your favorite characters from this book and put them together in a story of your own.

   • Take one of these old stories and set it in modern times. To get ideas, read Alvin Schwartz's two noodlehead collections, *All of Our Noses Are Here and Other Noodle Tales* and *There is a Carrot in My Ear and Other Noodle Tales* (see following bibliography). He has taken a lot of these old stories and told them as if they had happened to a family of noodleheads called the Browns.

   • Interview family members or friends. Tell them one or more of these stories and then ask what kind of "noodlehead" things they have done. Their answers may give you ideas for more stories. You can also, of course, think of foolish things *you* have done.

   • Write a newspaper account of the exploits of a noodlehead in one or more of the stories in this book.

   • Choose one of the noodlehead stories and illustrate it as a comic book.

   • Make a "Wanted" poster for a noodlehead character describing his or her misdeeds.

   • Write a "Dear Ann Landers" letter from a relative of one of the noodle-heads in this book. Describe the difficulties brought on by the noodle-head character.

If you come up with a good noodlehead story, send it to us. We may be interested in having other kids tell it or including it in a future book. Send your story via e-mail to: bnb@clarityconnect.com or via snail mail to:

Beauty & the Beast Storytellers
Martha Hamilton and Mitch Weiss
954 Coddington Road
Ithaca, NY 14850

Be sure to tell us how to contact you if we decide to use the story so that we can get written permission from you.

2. If you would like to read more noodlehead stories, check for these books at the library. Some may be hard to find, so ask your librarian for help.

Allard, Harry. *The Stupids Die*. Boston: Houghton Mifflin, 1981.

———. *The Stupids Step Out*. Boston: Houghton Mifflin, 1974.

———. *The Stupids Take Off*. Boston: Houghton Mifflin, 1984.

Berson, Harold. *Barrels to the Moon*. New York: Coward, McCann & Geoghegan, 1982.

Carrick, Malcolm. *The Wise Men of Gotham*. New York: Viking, 1973.

Denim, Sue. *The Dumb Bunnies*. New York: Scholastic, 1994.

Edwards, Roberta. *Five Silly Fishermen*. New York: Random House, 1989.

Ginsburg, Mirra. *The Twelve Clever Brothers and Other Fools: Folktales from Russia*. New York: J.B. Lippincott, 1979.

Jagendorf, Moritz A. *Noodlehead Stories From Around the World*. New York: Vanguard, 1957.

———. *The Merry Men of Gotham*. New York: Vanguard, 1950.

Leach, Maria. *Noodles, Nitwits, and Numskulls*. Cleveland: World, 1961.

Schwartz, Alvin. *All of Our Noses Are Here and Other Noodle Tales*. New York: Harper and Row, 1985.

———. *There is a Carrot in My Ear and Other Noodle Tales*. New York: Harper and Row, 1982.

Simon, Solomon. *More Wise Men of Helm and their Merry Tales*. New York: Behrman House, 1965.

———. *The Wise Men of Helm*. New York: Behrman House, 1945.

Singer, Isaac. *Naftali the Storyteller and His Horse, Sus*. New York: Dell, 1973.

———. *When Shlemiel Went to Warsaw and Other Stories*. New York: Dell, 1968.

Zemach, Margot. *The Three Wishes*. New York: Farrar, Straus, & Giroux, 1986.

3. If you would like more good stories to read and tell, see our award-winning books and recordings. *How and Why Stories: World Tales Kids Can Read and Tell* is available from August House Publishers in book, CD, and audiotape forms. *Stories in My Pocket: Tales Kids Can Tell* (book and audiotape) is available from Fulcrum Publishers (1-800-992-2908 or www.fulcrumresources.com). Those who teach storytelling will be interested in *Children Tell Stories: a Teaching Guide* (Richard C. Owen Publishers, 1-800-336-5588 or www.RCOwen.com). All of these items are also available through our website at:

    www.clarityconnect.com/webpages3/bnb/

    or by writing to us at the address on the previous page.

Story Sources

Most of the stories in this book are told in so many places around the world that it was often difficult to decide which story should come from which country. As Joseph Jacobs, the famous English folklorist, wrote, "It is indeed curious how little originality there is among mankind in the matter of stupidity." We made our decisions based on our desire to have as many different cultures represented as possible, as opposed to trying to reflect where a story may have originated or been told most often. Sometimes we added a motif from another country's variant in the interest of making a better story. At other times we shortened a story to make it a better length for telling or reading by children.

We have tried to avoid the use of foreign phrases or words that are hard to pronounce. From our experience, we've found that kids can understand and enjoy such words or phrases when they hear them explained in the context of a story, but they shy away from telling stories where the language doesn't feel comfortable to them.

The motifs referred to below are from *The Storyteller's Sourcebook: A Subject, Title, and Motif Index to Folklore Collections for Children* by Margaret Read MacDonald (Detroit: Gale, 1982) and *The Motif-Index of Folk-Literature* (Bloomington: Indiana University, 1966). Tale types are from *The Types of the Folktale* by Antti Aarne and Stith Thompson (Helsinki: Folklore Fellows Communication, 1961) and *A Guide to Folktales in the English Language* by D. L. Ashliman (New York: Greenwood, 1987).

The Boy Who Sold the Butter

The motif in this story is J1853.1, *Goods sold to object*. This is the first part of a longer story that we shortened to make it simple for children to read or tell. Other versions can be found in *Thirteen Danish Tales* by Mary C. Hatch (New York: Harcourt, Brace & World, 1947), *Picture Tales from Scandinavia* by

Ruth Bryan Owen (New York: Frederick A. Stokes, 1939), and *Noodlehead Stories from Around the World* by M.A. Jagendorf (New York: Vanguard, 1957).

Clever Elsie

This is tale type 1450, *Clever Elsie*. We have retold this tale freely. In order to make it simpler for children who choose to tell it, we did not include the search for three bigger fools that usually ensues. The German versions we consulted were *Folktales of Germany* by Kurt Ranke (Chicago: University of Chicago Press, 1966) and *Tales from Grimm* retold by Wanda Gag (New York: Coward-McCann, 1936).

Dead or Alive?

This very common story is tale type 1313A, *Prediction of death taken seriously*. The motifs are J2133.4, *Numskull cuts off tree limb on which he is sitting;* J2311.1, *Numskull is told he will die when his horse breaks wind three times;* and J2311.4, *The dead man speaks up.*

We found versions of this story from Uruguay, India, Russia, Turkey, Ethiopia, Italy, Poland, Switzerland, and Turkmenistan. Although we chose Uruguay as the source, we also used elements from the Indian version found in W.A. Clouston's *The Book of Noodles* (London: Elliot Stock, 1888). A version from Uruguay can be found in *The King of the Mountains: A Treasury of Latin American Folk Stories* by M.A. Jagendorf and R.S. Boggs (New York: Vanguard, 1960).

The Donkey Egg

The tale type in this story is 1319, *Fool thinks pumpkin is a horse's egg*. The motif is J1772, *Pumpkin thought to be an ass's egg*. We adapted this Algerian version from W.A. Clouston's *The Book of Noodles* (London: Elliot Stock, 1888). We also found versions from France, Switzerland, Russia, India, the United States, and China.

The Farmer Who Was Easily Fooled

The tale type here is 1529, *Thief claims to have been a donkey*. The motif is K403, *Thief claims to have been transformed into an ass*. A Lebanese version, "The Donkey Who Hit His Mother," may be found in *Two Fools and a Faker: Three Lebanese Folktales* retold by Gloria Skurzynski (New York: Lothrop, Lee, and Shepard, 1977). In addition to the Lebanese tale, the motif indexes cite versions from Spain, the Philippines, Switzerland, England, Morocco, Arabia, Ireland, and Israel.

The Fool's Feather Pillow

This story is tale type 1290B, *Sleeping on a feather*. It includes motif J2213.9, *Numskull finds that one feather makes a hard pillow, thinks a sackful would be unbearable.* An Irish version, "The Fool and the Feather Mattress," can be found in *Folktales of the Irish Countryside* by Kevin Danaher (New York: David White, 1970).

The Hunter of Java

The motif in this story is J2061.3, *Air-Castle: to sell hide of sleeping deer.* Versions can be found in *Studies in Religion, Folklore, and Custom in North Borneo and the Malay Peninsula* by I.H.N. Evans (London: Cambridge, 1923), *Kantchil's Lime Pit and Other Stories from Indonesia* by Harold Courlander (New York: Harcourt, Brace, 1950), and *Indonesian Legends and Folktales* by Adèle DeLeeuw (New York: Nelson, 1961). Courlander says variants of the story are commonly known throughout the Indonesian archipelago and on the Asiatic mainland. We chose Java, home of one of Courlander's informants, to make it simpler to have the audience join in in answer to the recurring question. (It's easier to pronounce Java as opposed to Sumatra and Malaya.) We also changed the name so as to allow for the rhyme in the audience participation part. We were assured by an Indonesian that "Ali bin Bavah" would be an appropriate name. ("Bin" means "son of" and is commonly found in Indonesian names.)

I'd Laugh, Too, If I Weren't Dead

This story is made up of two tale types: 1406, *The merry wives' wager,* and 1313, *The man who thought himself dead.* Motifs included are K1545, *Wives wager as to who can best fool her husband;* J2311.0.1, *Wife makes her husband believe he is dead;* and J2312, *Naked person made to believe that he is clothed.* We relied on two Icelandic versions of this story: "Who Was the Foolishest?" by Andrew Lang from *The Brown Fairy Book* (London: Longmans, Green & Co., 1904) and "Now I Should Laugh, If I Were Not Dead" from *Icelandic Legends* collected by Jón Arnason (London: Longmans, Green & Co., 1866).

Juan Bobo and the Pot That Would Not Walk

This is tale type 1291A, *Three-legged pot sent to walk home.* The motif is J1881.1.3, *Three-legged pot sent to walk home.* Stith Thompson cites variants from England, France, Spain, India, and the United States (Missouri). Puerto Rican versions can be found in *Greedy Mariani and Other Folktales of the Antilles* by Dorothy Sharp Carter (New York: Atheneum, 1974), *The Tiger and the Rabbit and Other Tales,* (by Pura Belpre) (Eau Claire, WI: E.M. Hale, 1946), and *The Three Wishes: A Collection of Puerto Rican Folktales* by Ricardo E. Alegria (New York: Harcourt, Brace & World, 1969).

The King Brought Down by One Blow

The motifs here are Z49.6, *Trial among the animals,* and N333.1, *Person killed by hitting fly on face.* We adapted the story from "A Tyrant" in Dean Fansler's

Filipino Popular Tales, American Folklore Society, Memoir 12 (1921): 388–389. Stith Thompson cites Indian and Japanese variants as well.

The Man Who Didn't Know What *Minu* Meant

The motifs included in this story are J2496.1, *"I don't know" thought to be a person's name*, and J1802.1, *"I don't understand."* We found versions in *West African Folk Tales* by W.H. Barker and Cecilia Sinclair (George G. Harrap, 1917), *The Cow-Tail Switch and Other West African Stories* by Harold Courlander and George Herzog (New York: Holt, Rinehart, and Winston, 1947), and *Tales from Africa* by Lila Green (Morristown, NJ: Silver Burdett, 1979).

The Mayor's Golden Shoes

The motifs here are J1703, *Town of fools*, and F823.1, *Golden shoes*. Versions of the story can be found in *A Treasury of Jewish Folklore* by Nathan Ausubel (New York: Crown, 1948), *More Wise Men of Helm and Their Merry Tales* by Solomon Simon (New York: Behrman House, 1965), and *Noodlehead Stories* by M.A. Jagendorf (New York: Vanguard, 1957).

The Men with Mixed-Up Feet

The tale types here are 1288, *Fools cannot find their own feet*, and 1289, *Each wants to sleep in the middle*. The principal motif is J2021, *Fools cannot find their own legs*. A version from Russia can be found in *The Twelve Clever Brothers and Other Fools: Folktales from Russia* by Mirra Ginsburg (New York: J.B. Lippincott, 1979). Similar stories can be found in *Folktales of Mexico* by Americo Paredes (University of Chicago Press, 1970), *Watermelons, Walnuts, and the Wisdom of Allah and Other Tales of the Hoca* by Barbara Walker (Parents Magazine Press, 1967), *Zlateh the Goat and Other Stories* by Isaac Bashevis Singer (New York: Harper & Row, 1966), and *The Book of Noodles* by W.A. Clouston (London: Elliot Stock, 1888).

Next Time I'll Know What to Do

This is tale type 1696, *What should I have said?* It includes motif J2461.1, *Literal following of instructions about actions*, and H341.3, *Princess brought to laughter by foolish action of hero*. Variations of this story are found in many countries throughout the world. English versions, known as "Lazy Jack," may be found in *Popular Rhymes and Nursery Tales of England* by James O. Halliwell (London: John Russell Smith, 1849) and *English Fairy Tales* by Joseph Jacobs (New York: G.P. Putnam's Sons, 1898). Our version has evolved from telling it over the years. In the original English version, Jack gets to marry the rich man's daughter and thus becomes a rich gentleman. By giving Jack the donkey and the two bags of gold instead, he is faced with the dilemma of how to carry them home and shows that he *can* think for himself. Though we feel it's important to be true to a culture and don't generally like to change endings, we feel the story doesn't suffer as a result of the changes we made.

The Ninny Who Didn't Know Himself

The motif in this story is J2012.4, *Fool in new clothes does not know self*. The tale type is 1284, *Fool does not know himself*. A version from Moldova was found in *The Twelve Clever Brothers and Other Fools: Folktales from Russia* by Mirra Ginsburg (New York: J.B. Lippincott, 1979). Clouston describes a similar Greek story in *The Book of Noodles* (London: Elliot Stock, 1888) as well as the Iranian version we summarized in "About the story."

No Doubt about It

Versions of this story were found in *Flowers from a Persian Garden* by W.A. Clouston (London: David Nutt, 1890) and *Fables From Afar* by Catherine T. Bryce (New York: Newson & Co., 1910).

Scissors!

The two main tale types in this story are 1365A, *Wife falls into a stream*, and 1365B, *Cutting with the knife or the scissors*. Versions of this story were told throughout Europe and North America. A Norwegian version was collected by Peter Christen Asbjørnsen and Jørgen Moe in *Tales From the Fjeld* (New York: G.P. Putnam's Sons, 1908).

Seven Foolish Fishermen

This story has the tale types 1287, *Fools cannot count themselves*; 1336, *Fool does not recognize own reflection*; and 1250, *A human well rope*. The motifs include J2031, *Counting wrong by counting oneself*, and J2031.1, *Numskulls count selves by sticking their noses in the sand*. This tale is found in many forms around the world. One French version, "The Tale of the Seven Brothers in the Well," can be found in *A Treasury of French Tales* by Henri Pourrat (Boston: Houghton Mifflin, 1954). Another French version with many of the same elements can be found in *Picture Tales From the French* by Simone Chamoud (Philadelphia: J.B. Lippincott, 1933). A picture book that tells a similar story is *Five Silly Fishermen* by Roberta Edwards (New York: Random House, 1989).

Such a Silly, Senseless Servant

We have put these three vignettes from Chinese folklore together into one tale. The first, stealing the rope, is motif K188, *Stealing only a small amount*. Versions can be found in "Celestial Humor, Selections from the *Hsiao Lin Kuang or Book of Laughter and Reminiscences*," by G. Taylor in *The China Review* 14 (1885–86): 85 and in *Quips from a Chinese Jest-Book* by Herbert A. Giles (Shanghai: Kelly & Walsh, 1925). The story of the hidden hoe is related to motif J2356, *Fool's talking causes himself and companions to be robbed*. It can be found in W.A. Clouston's *The Book of Noodles* (London: Elliot Stock, 1888). The last anecdote, that of the mismatched boots, falls under motif J2665, *The awkward servant*. Versions can be found in G. Taylor, "Humor of the Chinese Folk," *Journal of American Folklore* 36 (1923): 32 and in *The Dragon Book* by E.D. Edwards (London: William Hodge & Co., 1938).

What a Bargain!
This tale includes the motifs J2087, *The persuasive auctioneer*, and J2083, *The foolish attempt to cheat the buyer*. An Arabian version can be found in W.A. Clouston's *The Book of Noodles* (London: Elliot Stock, 1888).

When Giufà Guarded the Goldsmith's Door
The tale types here are 1009, *Guarding the door by carrying it away*, and 1653A, *Securing the door*. The tale is widely known throughout Europe and parts of the Middle East. An Italian version is mentioned in *The Book of Noodles* by W.A. Clouston (London: Elliot Stock, 1888). Another version can be found in *Italian Folktales* by Italo Calvino (New York: Harcourt Brace, 1980).

Whose Horse is Whose?
The motif in this story is J2722, *Telling their horses apart*. We retold the story from fragments found in "More About the Little Moron" by Herbert Halpert in *The Hoosier Folklore Bulletin* 2 (1943) and "A Comparative Study of the Folktales of England and North America" by E.W. Baughman, Indiana University dissertation, 1954.

The Wise Fools of Gotham
The motif in this story is J1703, *Town of fools*, along with tale types 1242A, *Carrying the load to spare the horse*; 1310, *Drowning an eel*; and 1213, *The pent cuckoo*. This is retold from W.A. Clouston's *The Book of Noodles* (London: Elliot Stock, 1888) and James O. Halliwell's *The Merry Tales of the Wise Men of Gotham* (London: John Russell Smith, 1840) as well as numerous other sources.